MW01257479

Death of the Dean

*For Brenda
and Sandy*

Marie Saunders

MARIE SAUNDERS

For Bill
Love of My Life,
Always

Chapter 1

I struggled with the key to the Liberal Arts building. The cold wind at my back was sharp, and snow fell in a swirling shower, numbing my fingers. I glanced at the empty parking lot where I had parked my Honda and wondered briefly if it had been wise to come alone to the campus so late at night.

Both Tess, my cat, and my Aunt Grace, my Southern Baptist aunt, had been against it. Tess had shown her disdain by ignoring her food and staring long and hard at me when I was putting on my coat. Aunt Grace had called just as I was leaving and said, "Since you didn't go to church this morning you need to stay home and read your Bible tonight." I hadn't argued with either one. I'd rubbed Tess on her tummy and promised Aunt Grace to read a chapter of Genesis when I got back.

I shivered from the cold, jerked the glove off my right hand to get a better grip and twisted the key one more time. The lock turned, and I shouldered the door open. I pushed inside, grateful for the rush of warm air that enveloped me and for the comforting glow of the hallway lights.

The barracks building that temporarily housed the Liberal Arts College was not a particularly comforting retreat during an Oklahoma snow storm. I certainly would not have been there except that the spring schedule was due in the Dean's office at 9 a.m. tomorrow and I had no intention of facing the Dean's wrath by being late with it.

I blew on my fingers as I walked quickly down the hall. I passed the Dean's office and noted that the lights were on. I heard the sound of his deep voice and I thought, *he's talking on the phone, probably dazzling his latest conquest.*

I smiled to myself and muttered, "Wonder if it's a woman

or a man." It was a longstanding rumor that Dean Phillip Stafford had a sex life as complicated as the Oklahoma weather. No one knew for sure if his preference was male or female, but that he was sexually active was certainly not in doubt.

I paused at my office, looked at my name "Connie Crashaw, Ph.D. Chairperson, English Department" centered on the door, and I remembered how shocked and pleased I had been when Dean Stafford had appointed me as the first female chairperson in the Liberal Arts College of our exclusive Harding University.

My pleasure had been short-lived, however, when I realized that the Dean's purpose had been self-serving. He had appointed me because he planned to control me, and the English department through me. After my first year, and a few violent encounters with him, I realized that he was a tyrant, and the only way I would survive was to knuckle under and do what he said.

I walked inside, took off my coat, and sat down at my desk. I sighed, and turned on the computer. Then I continued the task of scheduling classes and professors. This was the part of the chairperson's job that I hated the most. It was impossible to please everybody in the department, and as I glanced over the roster, I wondered which of my colleagues would take greatest offense at the schedule I had been working and reworking for the last two weeks.

I knew that Boyd Finnell would be upset when he saw that I had given him 18th century English poetry again. He hated to teach it, but he had to teach at least one graduate class, and this one was difficult. I fretted over Chris Herndon's whole schedule. Where could I put him in rooms close enough together to keep him from dashing out for a quick drink and coming back to class drunk? There were others I was worried about for various reasons, and I was finding it difficult to concentrate on the task.

My thoughts kept wandering back to the Dean. I could still hear the voices, louder now. I recognized the Dean's deep voice, sounding very angry. *He's* at *it again; some poor devil is catching hell!* I strained to hear the other voice, but I could not recognize who it was; I couldn't even be sure if it was male or female. The argument continued for another five minutes. Then I heard the sound of footsteps moving quickly down the tile hall. *It's either a discarded lover or a demolished professor leaving.*

God, what a piece of work the Dean is!

I had tensed my shoulders so much that the muscles in my neck were tighter than violin strings of a concert violinist. I deliberately relaxed and turned my attention to the paper labyrinth on the desk, determined to do what I had come out to do. But the wind whistling around the building like some wild banshee made me more nervous than ever.

I picked up the telephone on my desk. *I'll call Matt and ask him to meet me at Fanny's at 11:00. That will give me a goal and I'll get this damn schedule finished.* Matt was my closest friend on the faculty, and no matter how cantankerous and spiteful the other profs were, I could count on Matt for a smile and a joke.

Then I remembered. Matt had called me early in the evening to say that he would be in Tulsa, working with his friend Tony Lucas on a paper they were co-authoring. He wouldn't be home until late.

I slipped the phone back on its cradle and stood up. *I'll get a cup of coffee out of the machine. It's terrible stuff but at least it will be hot! And a shot of caffeine might be just what I need!* I walked out and headed for the bank of machines halfway down the hall. I heard a sound and looked up to see Clarence, the school janitor, on the second floor foyer looking down at me. I waved and called out, "Hi, Clarence, not a good night for us to be out!"

Clarence is slightly retarded, and the most I usually get out of him is a foolish grin and a few grunted words. But tonight he was in a mood to talk. He called out, "I sure hope you didn't have no trouble getting into the building tonight, Ma'am." His eyes were magnified into saucers by the thick lenses he wore.

Would I have had trouble, Clarence?" I asked, knowing what was coming.

Clarence blinked twice, sniffed, looked both ways down the hallway, hitched up his jeans with a mammoth pull at his belt. "The winds is a joining!" he said.

"Moving together, are they?"

"Yes, Ma'am. They're fierce tonight."

According to Clarence, the changing Oklahoma winds, coming from the south and then abruptly changing to the north, joined together in some mysterious way and caused differences in

3

pressure between the air inside and outside the building. These 'winds a joining' caused all sorts of havoc: stuck doors, overturned canisters, piles of dust on floors and window ledges. Clarence's joining winds was something of a joke among the faculty, who saw them as Clarence's excuse for not being able to keep up with the work that the old building required of its janitor.

"Come to think of it," I said, "I almost couldn't get my key to work in the east door tonight."

Clarence nodded fiercely. "Yep. The winds is a joining. You be careful with them doors, Dr. Crashaw. They're heavy, and when one of them contrary winds gets a hold of you, it's like a big old knife. I seen one like to take my hand off once." And he held up his hand to show me. "It was back about two . . . maybe three years ago. . . "

"Listen, Clarence," I interrupted, "I've got to get back to work, but I appreciate the warning. I'll sure look out for the winds a joining." I smiled at him and walked down the hall. That was the only way to escape from Clarence when he was in a talkative mood.

"You just watch out, Ma'am," Clarence called after me. I looked back to see him crush his stained cowboy hat more firmly on his head and mutter something to himself. I had to smile. Clarence was harmless, and he was always working hard at keeping the barn like building clean. I was glad he was there tonight. His presence was comforting.

I got the coffee, took a sip, grimaced. It was as bad as I had thought it would be. The lights were still on in the Dean's office, and I made a quick decision. *I'll take him a cup of coffee, commiserate with him for having to be out on a night like this, and maybe, just maybe, he'll be over his anger with me over my comment about that stupid Ten Year Plan fiasco.*

I had infuriated the Dean because I had laughed at his request for a projected Ten Year Plan for the English department. I had thought it was another stupid request he had simply passed on from Administration, but it had turned out to be his own special project. This I found out after I had gone into his office to tell him how ridiculous the whole thing was.

His face had flushed, and he had raged at me for fifteen minutes. The worse thing was that he had ended the tirade by writing a reprimand for insubordination to place in my file.

4

He's a bastard, but he is the Dean, and it's better to soothe him now, otherwise the next semester will begin, and he'll still have a chip on his shoulder and only God knows what he might do.

I went through the outer office which was his secretary's office and warily approached his office door. It was standing slightly ajar. I transferred both cups of coffee to one hand and knocked lightly. No response. I knocked again, harder this time. Still nothing. I took a deep breath, pasted a smile on my face, and gently pushed open the door.

I stopped dead in my tracks. The room was a wreck. Papers were strewn over the floor, the file cabinet was open, and files were scattered as if a tornado had blown through. A framed picture was lying on the floor with the glass smashed. The Dean was lying on the floor beside it, crumpled on his side, one leg sprawled at an awkward angle.

My heart was pounding wildly. I felt a rush of adrenalin, and the cups of coffee flew from my hand as if they had a life of their own. I heard a shocked voice crying, "My God, Oh My God, Oh My God," and only vaguely realized it was my own.

My first thought was that the Dean must have suffered a heart attack. I moved toward him, knelt at his side, and only then did I see the thin wire embedded in his neck like a child's tiny red ribbon.

I panicked. As I turned to run, I almost bumped into Clarence who was standing in the open doorway, his face rigid with fear. He seemed glued to the floor, but when I grabbed his arm, he jerked away, and I saw his dull eyes fill with fright.

"Lordy," said Clarence, his voice trembling, "Lordy, Lordy. It's the winds. . ." He stared at me.

I reached out and got his arm again. I took a couple of deep breaths to slow my pounding heart and steady my voice. I said, "Clarence, you've got to help me. I think the Dean is dead." I kept my eyes fixed on his and said, slowly and deliberately, "We've got to call the Campus police, and you've got to stay right here with me. Do you understand?"

I let my breath out in relief as he nodded and pulled his Stetson down further on his ears. I moved out of the Dean's office into the outer office, and picked up the telephone. My legs suddenly seemed like water and I slumped down on the secretary's desk.   My fingers were trembling so badly I was barely able to dial the 1-2-3-4 number.

I looked at Clarence who stood slumped over against the wall, his faded jeans hanging precariously from his hips.   He stared back at me, his jaws working rhythmically around the chew of tobacco he had just put in his mouth.   I bit down on my upper lip to stifle a hysterical cry.

On the third ring, a crisp voice responded, "Campus Security, Officer Pollock speaking."

"This is Connie Crashaw in the Liberal Arts building." I said.   "I need your help.   I think Dean Stafford is dead."

Chapter **2**

It seemed an eternity after I called campus police before anyone arrived, but it was actually only a few minutes before a young man in the campus police uniform dashed into the building. He looked vaguely familiar.

His name tag said "Patterson," and I remembered that I had a Patterson in my English Literature survey class a year ago. I told him what had happened and pointed him toward the Dean's office, then waited in the secretary's office, trying to keep my legs from wobbling out from under me.

When he came back out, his face was pale, and he was swallowing rapidly. I started to suggest that he might sit down, but he took a couple of deep breaths and said, "The Dean's dead all right." He shifted nervously from one foot to the other and said, "You didn't touch anything, did you, Ma'am?"

"No," I said. I leaned back against Nora's desk, which steadied me a bit. I added, "I . . . I dropped my coffee cup . . . I dropped two coffee cups. . . and I knelt down beside him."

"Just as long as you didn't touch anything," he said, his eyes darting from me to Clarence. "I called the City police department; they should be here any minute."

Clarence suddenly shuffled over to the secretary's desk, picked up a paper cup, and spat a stream of tobacco juice in it. My stomach heaved, and I swallowed desperately.

It was bad enough to toss two cups of coffee all over the pale green carpet. I didn't want to throw up on it too. I said, "For God's sake, Clarence, get rid of that tobacco."

He looked at me as if I had said something about his mother's origin. He hitched up his pants and stalked out of the room, his cowboy boots clomping dully on the carpet. Seeing the

Dean lying there seemed to be even harder on him than on me. He had gone into a kind of shock, and I regretted coming down on him about the tobacco.

The door opened and two men entered the room.

"I'm Detective Jacob Fleshman," the taller one said. "From the Oklahoma City Police Department. "This is my assistant, Sgt. Welston." Welston nodded, and Fleshman continued, "We understand there's been someone killed?"

"In there," I stammered, pointing to the Dean's office. I stood aside. I wasn't about to go back into the room. I was having trouble breathing and my pulse was hammering.

Detective Fleshman stood in the doorway, his sharp blue eyes focused directly on me which made me nervous. I had a feeling his eyes didn't miss much. He said, "Is this how you found him?"

"Yes," I said. I swallowed to get rid of the knot that had formed in my throat and glanced into the room again. I shouldn't have. The Dean's eyes, set in his face like black marbles, stared back at me.

I felt my legs turning weak again. Fleshman moved, laser fast, and caught me. He propelled me toward a chair. "Put your head down," he commanded.

I felt like a fool, but I jammed my head down between my knees and took several deep breaths. I am not a fainter, but here I was swooning like some Victorian maiden whose corset was too tight. The blood finally returned to my head, and I said, "I'm okay."

"Good." He sat down in a chair directly in front of me. I caught the faint fragrance of cologne and glimpsed a gun under his jacket. The combination seemed incongruous. Cologne and a gun? His smile was warm, but his eyes were cool and appraising. "Do you mind a few questions?"

I minded. I didn't want to answer any questions. What I wanted to do was go home, toss off a stiff drink, crawl into bed, pull the covers over my head, and wake up to find all this was a terrible nightmare. But I had a feeling this Detective wouldn't buy that scenario, so I nodded at him.

He said, "Why were you here tonight?"

"I had a deadline to meet for the spring schedule."

"Did you see the Dean earlier? Before he was killed?"

"No. He was in his office, but I didn't see him."

"Did you hear anything? Any sound of a struggle?"

"No. I heard him talking to someone, and they were arguing. I couldn't tell who it was."

"Was it a man or a woman?"

"I couldn't say for sure."

My mind was galloping off in another direction. I was thinking that the person who killed the Dean had walked past my office on the way out. I shuddered. What if I had been in the hallway? I shook my head, trying not to be afraid. I realized the detective was saying something more to me.

"Would you look around the Dean's office? Tell me if you see anything unusual, anything out of the ordinary?"

I didn't want to do what he was asking but I realized I really didn't have any choice. I gritted my teeth and stepped inside, not wanting to look at the body lying there.

Trying to keep my eyes averted, I glanced around the room. The Dean's huge oaken desk stood squarely in the middle of the room. Behind it, his brown leather chair lay overturned on its side. His credenza and two file cabinets which lined up on the wall behind the desk had been rummaged through. The contents of both were strewn on the floor.

A bouquet of bronze and white mums, apparently from the credenza, had been crushed into the carpet. The bookcases, full of leather bound books, which stretched across the other side of the room had not been touched.

"See anything?"

I didn't see anything except mass confusion, but I said, "He always keeps his credenza locked."

He moved into the room, stood beside the Dean's body. I shut my eyes. "What about these?" He was holding several rainbow-colored condoms in his hand.

I felt my mouth pop open in amazement. I stammered, "I don't know." Then, for no sensible reason, I asked, "Where did you find them?"

"Under the Dean's body."

My brain was going into overdrive, and I was getting more and more anxious to get out of the room. The metallic odor of the blood, coupled with the musky smell of the crushed mums was about to make me ill.

I said," Well, I don't know anything about them. I can't help you. May I please get out of here?"

"Sure," he said. I guess he was afraid I was going to faint on him. He handed the condoms to Weston and said, "Bag them."

He took my arm, guided me back into the secretary's office and shut the door behind him. Then he asked, "Are you all right? Can I get you coffee? Water?"

"No, "I said. "It was the smell. It was getting to me."

He smiled again. "I understand." He paused. "Do you feel up to few more questions?"

"Give me a minute," I said, "This has been quite a shock."

He helped me into a chair, pulled one up beside me and waited patiently. I took a few deep breaths, straightened my shoulders and said, "I'm okay now, go ahead."

He asked, "'When you arrived, did you notice anything, anyone in the parking lot?

"No, but I wasn't paying attention. I was hurrying to get inside. But I did notice that some cars were parked by the field house, a short distance away. I think a basketball game was going on."

"Who did you see when you got inside the building?"

"I saw Clarence, the maintenance man. No one else."

He got up and began to pace around the floor. I noticed that his suit was well cut, maybe an Armani. His shoes looked as if they had been spit polished. He said, "Did the Dean have enemies?"

My mind was beginning to move into normal mode once again, and his question was a bit disconcerting. The answer would be to suggest who might have a motive for murdering the Dean. I tried to equivocate. "I'm sure he did. Most of us do."

The Detective's mouth tightened ever so slightly. He said, "Do you know anyone who would want him dead?"

I was getting very tired, and I was about to say that I knew at least fifty people who hated him and would be glad that he was dead. Fortunately I was spared from making that mistake.

Vice Pesident Munsell strode into the room. He said, "I just heard about Dean Stafford. Are you all right, Dr. Crashaw?"

"Yes," I said. For once I was glad to see Munsell. He was not one of my favorite people, but he could take over this miserable situation, and I could get out of here. Or so I thought.

Munsell turned to Fleshman. "I'm Vice President Munsell. I was working in my office when I got the call from the campus police." He paused. "This is a terrible thing, simply terrible."

Fleshman said, "You were in your office? Where?"

"In the Administration Building, across campus."

"Were you here all evening?"

Munsell's voice was impatient. "Yes, since seven o'clock. But more important, what are you doing about all this?"

Fleshman's voice was cool and he didn't bristle at Munsell's tone. He said, The Medical Examiner is on the way, and we have secured the crime scene."

He turned his back on Munsell and said to me, "Is there next of kin who should be notified?"

Munsell resented anyone ignoring him. He answered before I could. He said, "His wife., that is, his ex-wife, Helen Stafford, should be notified."

Fleshman was still directing his questions to me. He said, "Where does she live?"

Munsell, his face mottled, moved around to face Fleshman. He said, "She lives near the campus. Mrs. Stafford is a part time professor in Dr. Crashaw's department. I'm sure Dr. Crashaw will be willing to go and tell her what has happened."

I barely managed to stifle a gasp. I couldn't believe that Munsell was passing the buck to me. I had no desire to face Helen Stafford. She did not rate very high on my popularity scale. She was as despicable in her own way as the Dean.

Five years ago she had dumped the Dean for a student ten years her junior. She had flaunted her young man before the Dean and the rest of the University community, deliberately, I thought, to embarrass the Dean and make him as miserable as she could.

Helen was not a good person, and I didn't want to be the one to tell her that her ex-husband was dead. That task was not in my job description. I said, "I'd rather not, Dr. Munsell. I'd really like to go home."

Munsell ran a hand over his thinning hair and fixed me with his pale brown eyes. "It would be easier for her if a woman is there. To lend support in her grief."

He sounded like a pious TV evangelist. I started to say

"She won't be grieving, believe me" but I caught myself in time.

There was a hint of a threat in his voice when he replied, "Since you are her Chairperson . . ." His voice trailed off.

An alarm went off in my head. *This is your boss, and don't forget it. He's also the one who will appoint the new Dean. Don't be stupid.* All right," I said, editing the annoyance out of my voice.

Fleshman had been standing slightly back of Munsell while this exchange was going on. He moved toward me and said, "If you like, you can ride with me."

I was glad for his offer. I didn't feel like driving my car, and his presence would be a great relief to me. Telling Helen would not be easy. I heard the winds whistling around the windows and thought of Clarence and what he had said about the winds a'joining. They had sure played hell tonight.

Chapter **3**

I watched the snow flakes, wet and fat, slap against the windshield of the police car. I was irritated that I had let myself be manipulated into being the one who brought the bad news to Helen. *Messengers often get killed, and Helen Stafford is not a nice person. I should have told Munsell to bug off and do the job himself.* I glanced at Fleshman, noticing for no particular reason how his dark hair, flecked with gray, curled over his coat collar.

Earlier, I had noticed and been impressed by his good grooming. Unconsciously I always check out anyone I meet, male or female, and evaluate them to a degree by how they dress. This practice was a throw back to my Aunt Grace's early instruction. She had constantly reminded me that a slovenly and ill kept outward appearance reflected poorly on the person. How many times had she solemnly laid that little adage on me?

She was particularly critical of a person's shoes. She said, "Always check out a man's shoes, Constance. Well shined shoes are the mark of an intelligent and decisive man -- the kind of man you need to be interested in." She hadn't bothered to explain the logic of her statement, and I hadn't had the inclination to challenge her.

Fleshman must have felt my eyes on him. He turned and said, "What do you teach?"

"English."

"Hum. For some reason I enjoyed English."

"You did?" I couldn't keep the surprise out of my voice. Most of my male students generally groaned when they were told that English was a required subject even in college. They would say, "I hate English, it's my worst subject."

Fleshman apparently caught the disbelief in my voice.

He said, "I guess it was because I had a good teacher. The grammar part always made sense to me. It's kind of like math, you know."

I was beginning to appreciate this man's insight. "It is," I said, "But not many people ever see that." I paused. "How do you feel about literature?"

"Ah, that's a little different. Literature was tougher. But, like I said, I had a good teacher. I learned to like T.S. Eliot."

I couldn't believe my ears. "Did you like his poetry?"

"Some of it. I couldn't understand The Waste Land, but I liked Prufrock. Sometimes I feel like him." He grinned, and said "I wonder if I dare to eat a peach."

I couldn't believe what I was hearing. He had not only read Eliot; he could quote a line from Prufrock which told me that he had some understanding of what Eliot was saying about modern society.

Now I was impressed. A cop who smelled good, looked good, and most importantly, liked literature.

He said, "Do you like your job?"

"Yes. I like the classroom and the students. The politics I can do without." I was thinking of Munsell.

"Politics in academia?" He sounded surprised.

It was my turn to laugh. "More than you can imagine. Political intrigue on a college campus makes D.C. politics look like small potatoes."

I was about to ask him where he had gone to college when we topped the last small hill before Helen's house. I pointed and said, "That's Helen's house just below." It was an old Victorian house crouched among a grove of large pin oak trees. Green and gold Christmas lights strung in the evergreen bushes along the curving drive gave the area a festive air.

I remembered when the Dean had started renovating the old house. He wanted to make it into a showplace where he could give elaborate parties for his socialite friends.

About three months after all the work had been completed, Helen dropped her bombshell on him. The way we heard it via the college grapevine was that she came home one day, walked into his office and said, "I'm in love with someone else. I want a divorce."

The someone else was a graduate student. She moved out

of the newly redecorated house and into a small apartment with her new love. They married within six months.

The Dean had been so devastated that he neither fought her over the divorce nor made any attempt to keep the house for himself. She and her young man moved into the house as soon as the Dean moved out. Their marriage had lasted another year, and then the young man moved on.

The Dean didn't easily get over losing Helen. He carried a torch for her for another year or so, and then began his own conquests. But it was my private opinion that he never really got completely over losing her.

Fleshman pulled up into the circular drive and parked. A lone electric light, shaped in the form of a lantern, only faintly illuminated the large wrap-around porch.

We got out of the car, and walked up to the doorway. I fumbled for the doorbell, finally found it, and heard the ripple of chimes. In a few minutes, a light flashed on in the hallway, and Helen called out, "Who is it?"

"It's me, Helen. Connie Crashaw."

She opened the door slightly and peered out. "For heaven's sake, what are you doing out in this weather?"

The wind had picked up and I was shivering from the cold. "Can we come in?"

Helen looked over my shoulder and saw Fleshman. A smile spread over her face. "Of course, bring your gentleman in out of the cold."

We stepped inside. I didn't bother to tell her that he wasn't my gentleman. I wanted to get through with this task, get out, and go home.

As always, Helen looked like she had just stepped out of Vogue magazine. A red velour warm up suit emphasized her trim figure and her healthy tan. She had pulled back her hair, a silvery blonde, and caught it up in a ponytail. She looked like a fashion model.

She fixed her gaze on Fleshman. I could almost see her mind working. She was wondering what I was doing in the company of such a good looking man.

I said, "This is Detective Fleshman."

She raised her eyebrows. "A Detective, Connie? I'm impressed." I recognized the glitter in her eyes. She had been drinking. Rather heavily, I imagined. I said, "He's an Oklahoma City Policeman, Helen."

Helen touched Fleshman's arm ever so lightly and said, "Let's go into the den; it's warmer there." I couldn't believe her nerve; she was coming on to Fleshman!

Fleshman must have seen the expression on my face. He gave me a quirky smile as if to say 'I know what's going on' and followed her into the den.

The fireplace in the tall ceilinged room burned brightly. The only other illumination came from one small table lamp and a dozen or more votive candles scattered around the room. Had we interrupted a lover's tryst? Was some young student, a new conquest perhaps, hiding upstairs?

Helen motioned for us to sit down. She stopped at the bar. "Would you care for a drink, Connie, Detective?"

I wanted a drink, but I knew that if I took one I'd probably fall on my face. The adrenalin rush I had experienced and the tension of the past two hours, coupled with a bourbon would do me in, so I said, "No, thanks."

Fleshman shook his head and remained standing.

"Then I'll have to drink alone." She splashed whiskey over ice and smiled brightly at Fleshman and added, "I find that depressing."

"Ms. Stafford," Fleshman began, "Maybe you had better sit down. I have some bad news about your husband, the Dean."

"My *ex-husband,* Detective," Helen said, taking a deep pull at her drink. "He's my *ex-husband.* What's he done now? Another young female felled by his fatal charms?"

Her voice slurred over the alliteration, and I knew she was drunker than I had thought. *Maybe this business of having young men as lovers isn't as great as Helen had dreamed it would be.*

Fleshman said, "Your ex-husband is dead, Mrs. Stafford." He was watching her intently.

"What?" She glanced from him to me, and I thought her surprise was genuine.

"Dr. Crashaw found him tonight in his office at the University."

She turned toward me. "My God, Connie, what happened? Did he have a heart attack?" Her face had paled and the glass in her hand trembled. She moved to the couch facing the fireplace and sat down. I was glad that Fleshman answered for me. "He was murdered, Mrs. Stafford."

"What do you mean, *murdered?* Who would murder Phil?"

He said, "That's what I'm trying to find out. That's why we are here."

Helen rolled the now empty glass between her hands and said, "How was he killed?"

"He was beaten to death." He paused and added, "Someone crushed his skull with a heavy instrument."

"Oh, my God," she said. "Poor Phil." I saw tears forming in her eyes, and for the first time since we had arrived, she seemed uncertain and upset. She stood up. "I need another drink."

"Maybe you'd better not, Ms. Stafford," said Fleshman. "I have to ask you some questions, and you need to answer them carefully."

He paused a moment, waiting I supposed for her to absorb the shock of what he had told her. He said, "Can you tell me where you were tonight? Between eight and ten o'clock?"

Her eyes widened. "You don't think *I* killed him? My God, that's absurd."

Fleshman didn't relent. He said, "Where were you, Ms. Stafford?"

Her voice chilled. "I've been here since eight thirty."

"From eight thirty on, you were here?"

"Yes."

"Alone?"

There was a nanosecond of silence before she answered. "Yes, I was alone."

I looked quickly at Fleshman. I wondered if he had detected the slight hesitation before she answered. I glanced around the room again. The candles were burning, and two large pillows lay to the left of the fireplace. No doubt about it, it was a nice setting for a romantic tryst.

Fleshman said, "Do you have any idea who might have killed your husband?"

"Of course not."

"Did the Dean have any enemy that you can think of who might want him dead?"

I could see her pulling herself together, straightening her shoulders. I had to admire her spirit. She was not going to let Fleshman catch her up in an admission of anything until she had time to absorb what he had told her.

She said, "Some people didn't like him. As Dean, he was responsible for everything that happened in the School of Liberal Arts. Sometimes that meant being tough, and shaking up some people. He did that. But I don't know anyone who hated him enough to kill him."

"Somebody did." Fleshman's voice was clear and firm.

Helen glanced toward the bar. It was apparent, to me at least, that she wanted us to leave so that she could have another drink -- maybe several other drinks. Or find solace in the arms of her young man, if he indeed were hidden upstairs.

Her reply was short and abrupt. "Then it would be good for you to start looking for the real murderer, Detective."

Fleshman said, "That is what I am doing, Ms. Stafford."
The tension between them flickered like heat lightning.

The whole scene was making me very uncomfortable. I decided that I had had enough pressure for the evening. I said, very deliberately, "I would like very much to go home, Detective Fleshman. If you're through here?"

He glanced at me and then back at Helen. "I'll be in touch, Ms. Stafford."

"You do that, Detective. Let me know as soon as you find out who murdered Phil." I thought she was being very foolish by using such an antagonist tone toward Fleshman. But then Helen was not known for her wisdom or for her diplomacy.

I said, "We'll let ourselves out."

The night air felt good. It was sharp, but fresh and invigorating. The snowing had stopped and a few stars had broken through the clouds.

Fleshman was silent as we pulled around the curved drive and back on to the snow packed road. I said, "She's not very pleasant when she's drinking."

He smiled slightly. "I'm used to dealing with unpleasant people. That's a part of my job."

He was silent for several moments, then he asked, "What kind of relationship did she have with the Dean?"

I thought for a moment. Defining their relationship was

as difficult as interpreting a canto by Ezra Pound, and just as complicated. What could I say? That the Dean apparently loved her more than she had loved him? That he had carried a torch for her for a time? That she had humiliated him by having an affair with a student while she was married to him?

I tried to be truthful and diplomatic. I said, "That's a far more complex question than I can answer. But as for now, I do know that the Dean was still interested in her welfare. I also think that both of them had moved on to other interests."

He said, "Did you notice the candles?" His eyes *were* good. My idea that he didn't miss much was proving true.

"Yes."

"Interesting."

I decided that I didn't have to comment on his 'interesting.' I moved ever so slightly over against the door and watched the darkened landscape spin by.

I was tired and I was worried. Somewhere out there was a murderer. A murderer who now knew that I had been in my office that night and that I would have seen him had I opened my door when I heard footsteps.

I shivered. I pulled my coat closer around me. I was not only cold, I was scared. It was not a comfortable feeling.

Chapter 4

I felt as if I had just closed my eyes when the phone jangled me awake at 6:00 a.m. It was Aunt Grace, who had heard on the news of the Dean's death and that I had found his body. She was frantic, and it took me several minutes to calm her down enough to assure her I was fine, not hurt in any way.

When she finally composed herself, her Baptist sense of right and wrong quickly came into play. "I'm so thankful you are all right, Constance. It's a terrible thing for someone to murder another human being. If you can do anything to bring this criminal to justice, you know you must do it."

"That's not my job, Aunt Grace. The Oklahoma City Police department will handle it."

"But if you can help, it's your duty to do so."

I smiled. Aunt Grace was being her usual bossy self. She had been issuing ultimatums since she had taken me in after my mother's death, a sad and rebellious teenager. I owed her, so I listened, interjecting an occasional "Yes, Aunt Grace."

What I didn't say was that I was staying as far away from the investigation as possible. Finally she said, "And what is the name of the detective in charge?"

"Jacob Fleshman, but . . . ." She had hung up.

I climbed out of bed. My head felt like it was stuffed with cotton, and I was jittery from lack of sleep. I got coffee and sat in the den, thinking about last night's events, and decided I had done the best I could with all that had happened. I moped around until 10:00 a.m. before I finally got away from the house.

It was cold and bleak outside which did nothing to lift my spirits. I was hungry, and I pulled into a near-by Hardees

Restaurant and went inside to get a bite to eat.

There were only a few customers since it was after breakfast and before lunch. I munched on a greasy egg and bacon biscuit, and replayed the night before.

After the encounter with Helen, Fleshman had driven me back to the University where Munsell was being his usual officious self. He had taken me aside and warned me about talking to the press.

I had assured him I would be very circumspect and refer everyone to him. I had learned a long time ago that if your boss has an ego that needs to be massaged, it's best to massage it, and Munsell had an ego as big as his hefty paunch.

It had been past midnight before I managed to get home, and that's when the horror of the whole evening had crashed in on me. I kept hearing the voices, and wracking my brain trying to identify the other voice. I couldn't. I still couldn't be sure it was a man or a woman.

The worst thing was how often the sight of the Dean sprawled out on the floor with his black eyes staring at me flashed back into my mind. How could anyone have hated him enough to kill him? To smash his head so brutally?

I thought about the things I should have done. I should have listened more carefully to the other person's voice. I should have walked to the Dean's office while the argument was going on. The Dean might still be alive.

Then another thought hit me. *I might have been the murderer's second victim.* He, or she, certainly would not have wanted me around to talk. I stared out the polished plate glass window of the restaurant at the leaden sky and I shivered. I sipped the hot coffee, putting off the return to University as long as I reasonably could.

I had no desire to talk to anyone about what had happened. I certainly didn't want to view the crime scene again. But I knew I had to go back, so after the caffeine from three cups of coffee had sufficiently primed me, I got up and stepped outside.

The wind seemed colder and the day darker than when I had left the house. I hurried to my car, and started off carefully on the icy street that led onto the campus parking lot. When I got there, I walked carefully toward the buildings.

Once inside the building, I hastened past the Dean's office. When I saw the yellow and black crime scene tape fixed across the door, the horror of the Dean's death hit me again and my stomach turned queasy. Would the sight of the Dean's body sprawled on the floor, his blood spilling from his crushed head, ever disappear?

Poor Nora, she's got to work in that office, I thought. *How will she handle what's happened to the Dean?*

My heels clicked, staccato-like, on the hard floor and I hastened down the hall, thinking about Nora. She was a good secretary and I liked her. She took no nonsense from anyone and handled both professors and students even-handedly and firmly. She was the one who kept the office of the Dean running smoothly.

I turned the corner to my office and almost bumped into to Lew Hawkins, the lanky chairperson of the Social Studies department. I wasn't too surprised to see him. Lew was an opportunist who was alert to make the most of any situation, and I was sure that the same thought had occurred to him that had occurred to me.

The Dean had been killed, and someone would have to be named to take his place. *It might as well be me* was probably running through Hawkins' mind just as it had been running through mine.

He managed a hint of concern when he said, "My God, Dr. Crashaw, I heard you were here when the Dean was killed."

"Yes," I said, and kept walking. "It was a shock to me." I did not want to talk to him about it.

But he was persistent; he caught my arm and asked, "Was there anybody else here but you?"

I kept walking and said, "Just me -- and Clarence."

Lew's eyes behind his glasses were owlish. He said, "Who do you think could have done this?"

I finally stopped, faced him, and said, "I don't know. That's the police department's job to find out, and I'm sure they will. Right now I've got work to do."

I left him standing in the hallway, gawking at me. I had trouble liking Lew. He was too deferential, too smooth and too ingratiating. He would be working whatever angles he could to be appointed as Dean. I unlocked the door to my office and slipped inside. I picked up the phone and dialed Matt. "Pick up the phone, Matt," I said under my breath. "I need to talk to you."

The phone was on its eighth ring when I heard a knock on the door. I was almost afraid to open it, thinking someone from the press would be there.

But it was Matt. He enveloped me in a bear hug and just held me for a long minute. Then he said, "I'm sorry you found the Dean; it must have been terrible." The concern in his voice was palpable and for the first time in twenty four hours, I felt I felt safe and secure.

Matt and I had become friends because he was someone outside the English department I could talk to about the craziness that went on within the department. He was a good listener and helped me keep things in perspective with his calm, reasonable responses. When Eric, whom I had loved so wildly and completely, had asked for a divorce, it was Matt who had helped me get over the initial shock, and stood by through the whole messy divorce. If not for Matt, I don't think I would have survived.

Now he was patting me on the shoulder and saying, "It's okay, Con, not the end of the world."

"It was awful, Matt, finding him like that. He looked like, he looked like . . ." I had begun to shake, and I thought I might begin blubbering like a baby.

Matt hugged me tighter and said, "Don't think about it, Connie."

I looked over his shoulder and saw Boyd Finnell standing in the doorway. I pushed back from Matt and moved to my desk, hating the slight smirk on Finnell's face.

"Hope I'm not interrupting anything," he said, the smirk now in his voice.

I wanted to slap him. Finnell was the senior English faculty member and an ever present thorn in my flesh. Under a thin veneer of pretended gentility, he was as vicious and dangerous as a diamond back rattler, and so paranoid that he imagined that everyone, students and faculty alike, was out to do him harm.

I personally thought he walked a thin line between sanity and insanity. I asked, "What do you need, Dr. Finnell?" I hated the tightening of my neck muscles and the tension in my gut that his mere presence caused.

His pale blue eyes flashed and he said, "I heard that our Dean is dead. Someone finally killed him?" I glanced up at Matt who had turned his back on Finnell and was busy looking out of the window. He didn't like Finnell any better than I did.

I said, "Yes, he is dead."

I didn't relish any long conversation with Finnell. I wanted to get rid of him as quickly as I could. But he wasn't ready to leave. He ran his hand over his sparse sandy hair, and his eyes darted nervously between Matt and me.

He said, "I heard somebody beat him up and bashed his head in." The venom in his voice was unsettling. He was actually *glad* the Dean was dead. I was not surprised. They despised each other and had got into shouting matches that had shaken the building. Finnell had a very short fuse, and that, coupled with his paranoia, hurtled him into frightening rages.

"What did you want to see me about, Dr. Finnell?" I wasn't going to listen to him chortle over the Dean's death. His face darkened. He knew I was trying to get rid of him.

"I thought you might have the spring schedules ready by now." His tone implied that I was derelict if I didn't.

I felt my anger rise. "Your schedule will be in your mailbox in a few days."

"For this semester I want two Freshman composition classes and a Seminar in Twain."

"I'll see what I can do." I struggled to keep my anger under control. I hated the way he could upset me just by being his obnoxious self.

"Then you and Professor Duncan have a nice day," he said as he turned around and walked out of the office. As I watched him go, my mind flew to the things I'd like to do to him. Like slash his tires, put sugar in his gasoline tank, smear black paint on the side of his precious red pickup truck. I took a couple of deep breaths and looked at Matt.

He was smiling. "Want me to bust his face? He's certifiably crazy, and I'd love to do it."

For a brief moment, I pictured Matt, trim and muscled, working over Finnell. It was a pleasant prospect.

Just then the telephone rang. I picked up the phone and immediately recognized the voice. It was a particularly persistent and obnoxious reporter from the <u>Daily Oklahoman</u>, a woman I didn't like.

I grimaced, and put my hand over the mouthpiece. "Don't go," I whispered to Matt. I didn't have the stamina to deal with this woman right now. She was known for her ruthless persistence in rooting out news, and for twisting the facts around so as to make a lurid story out of almost anything.

I quickly said "All questions concerning the Dean's death will be handled by Vice President Munsell," and put the phone back on its hook.

When the phone started ringing again, I motioned to Matt for us to leave. Once outside, I said, "That was a reporter, and I don't like her very much."

He looked at me, a sardonic smile on his face, and said, "I gathered as much, but someone will have to talk to the press."

"But thankfully, not me. Munsell told me to keep my mouth shut and let him handle the media." I smiled what I hoped was a satisfied smile and added, "And that is exactly what I intend to do." We had been walking down the hall, and I looked up to see Detective Fleshman approaching.

I said to Matt, "This is the Detective in charge. His name is Fleshman." When Fleshman reached us, I introduced Matt to him, and watched as they shook hands. Matt looked like a professor with his chinos and sweater and longish hair, but Fleshman didn't fit my idea of how a policeman should look. He was too well tailored, too well groomed, more like a CEO right out of a <u>Forbes</u> magazine.

Matt was saying, "It's a terrible thing -- the Dean's death."

"Yes," Fleshman said. "Murder is always terrible."

Matt responded quickly. He said, "Of course it is." But before those words had died in his mouth, he came out with a shocking and what seemed to me to be an inflammatory question. He said, "But is it ever defensible?"

I think the question caught Fleshman off guard, as it had me, but he was quick to respond. He said, "No, I don't think so, but then my job is not to determine about whether it a defensible act or not. That's what our courts do. My job is to catch the murderer."

I laughed nervously and said, in an attempt to derail, or

make less confronting Matt's question, which I thought was particularly foolish. "You have to know that Matt is a philosophy teacher, and he loves to provoke thought by asking provocative questions."

I wanted to shake Matt. I knew what he was doing. He wanted to get into a discussion with Fleshman, match wits with him, perhaps confuse him if he could, but I thought he was unwise to challenge someone he had just met and especially the detective in charge of a murder.

Fleshman's reply was short. "I understand."

Matt, in an apparent attempt to be a little less aggressive said, "I guess in your profession, you see a lot of murder and mayhem."

"More than I like to."

"Seems like a tough profession to be in."

"It pays off when I catch the bad guys."

"Do you always catch them?"

Fleshman smiled, a wintry kind of smile and said, "Usually I do. I ask questions and I follow leads and I do a lot of grub work, and, finally, I catch most of them."

He paused a second and said, "Do you mind if I ask you a few questions?"

This time Matt was caught off guard. I could hear the surprise in his voice. He said, "Of course not."

There was still a tension in the air. I intended later to chide Matt about taking on the Detective.

Then, for whatever reason, it seemed to me that Fleshman's voice became calm and relaxed. He said, "Can you tell me where you were last night between eight and ten o'clock"?

Matt's face reddened slightly, and he glanced at me. He said, "I was in Tulsa, working with another professor on a seminar paper we're co-authoring."

"Your friend's name?" Fleshman was writing in a small notebook. He looked up at Matt.

"Tony Lucas. He's on staff at Tulsa University."

"What time did you get back to Oklahoma City?"

"Around eleven or eleven-thirty, I'm not sure."

"Did anyone see you or meet you in Oklahoma City?"

Matt said, "No, I went right home."

"When was the last time you saw the Dean?"

Matt stared at Fleshman a moment before he answered. "I think I passed him in the hall Friday afternoon."

"But you didn't see him Sunday?"

"No." Matt's answer was emphatic.

"Any idea who might have killed him?"

"No."

"Know any enemy that might want him dead?"

"I didn't know his personal life that well, but no, as I said, I don't have any idea who would have killed him."

"But someone surely did. Want him dead, I mean."

"That's obvious, but I'm afraid I can't help you."

Fleshman's voice remained calm and professional. He said, "I'll want to talk to you again."

Matt shrugged and said, "Sure." He glanced at me, winked, and said, "I'll catch you later," and walked away.

I watched Matt stride down the hall, not looking back, and I said, "Being a Detective doesn't make you many friends, does it?"

Fleshman smiled wryly. "I thought maybe it was my grammar that bothered people. Then he added, 'Look, I'm a cop. I suspect everybody, and I ask questions. And some people don't like that."

"Do you suspect me?" I suppose I asked the question out of a nervous reflex, but I certainly didn't expect the question that he shot back at me.

"Did you do it?" His blue eyes were riveted on my face.

"No!" I stammered. "Of course not!" My mouth was suddenly dry, and I'm sure my face reflected shock. It had never entered my mind that I'd be a suspect.

He smiled and said, "No, I don't think you did. You wouldn't have killed the Dean and then stayed around. Or dumped two cups of coffee on that beautiful plush carpet."

I was feeling a bit exasperated because of the abruptness of his question and the emotional jolt it had given me. I said, "Well, I appreciate your vote of confidence." I hoped he would detect the sarcasm in my voice, but if he did, he chose to ignore it.

Instead he said, "But you and Clarence were here when it happened."

"Yes." I wondered what he was getting at.

"Then you and Clarence could be in danger."

That was a warning, and I was not ready for it. My mouth was dry again. "But why?" I asked. "I didn't see anything. I don't think Clarence did."

"You said you heard loud voices coming from the Dean's office that night. And you heard someone leaving soon after that."

"Yes, but I haven't the slightest idea who it was."

"But the murderer doesn't know that"

Now I *was* beginning to get nervous. The thought that I was in the building when the Dean had been killed was upsetting enough. Now I had to worry that he, or she, might think I knew more than I did.

I tried for a little humor. I said, "Maybe if I draped a large banner in the hallway saying 'I didn't see anything; I don't know anything about who murdered Dean Stafford,' and signed my name, I'd be okay?"

Fleshman didn't smile. He said, "It's possible that you might later remember something distinctive about the voices. Or the footsteps. Sometimes our subconscious dredges up things that we don't know are there."

I thought how hard I had tried last evening to recognize the other voice and how miserably I had failed. I was becoming more and more convinced that I didn't want to have anything more to do with this investigation. I wanted to get Fleshman's attention off of me. I said, "Have you talked to Clarence?"

"Briefly. He didn't make a lot of sense. Kept saying something about the winds and that he saw a tall sailor."

I was surprised. That was the first I had heard about a tall sailor. "You know Clarence has a problem?" I said quietly. I just didn't want to call Clarence retarded. In some ways he was smarter than a number of our brilliant professors who worked less and got paid much better.

Fleshman said, "I know. But I still want to talk to you and him together."

Before he could say anything else, Nora Tennyson, the Dean's secretary, came storming down the hallway. Her eyes were flashing, and her voice was furious. She looked like one of the furies in full flight.

"Dr. Crashaw," she said, her voice trembling with emotion, "If you don't get those men out of my way and that horrible Halloween tape from off the Dean's office, I intend to call the campus police and have them thrown out."

This was my chance to let someone else sound off. I turned to Fleshman,, barely managing to stifle a smile. I said, "This is the Dean's secretary, Nora Tennyson."

And to Nora I said, "This is Detective Fleshman, the Oklahoma City detective in charge."

I paused and added, "Your move, Detective Fleshman."

Chapter 5

I am not an ardent feminist, but there are times when I enjoy seeing a strong male being confronted by an equally strong *and* determined female. I'm always curious to see who blinks first.

Nora said, "Your men will not get out of the Dean's office so that I can straighten his files and records and bring some kind order out of this chaos. Can you do something about it?"

Her eyes nailed him in their intensity. I almost laughed. Nora was smart, and she was using a familiar ploy, one I had seen her use countless times with distressed students and irate professors alike. She attacked first and threw them off their stride, got them confused and unsure, and before they realized what was happening, she was in control of the situation.

Fleshman took a different tack. He smiled back at her, a disarming smile which showed his even white teeth. He said, "I'm sure I can. And I will. But I'd like to ask you a few questions, and check the crime scene one more time with you and Dr. Crashaw."

The fire went out of her eyes, and she managed a slight smile. His poise and gentleness had disarmed her. I had been so busy admiring how smoothly he was handling Nora that I had not noticed how cleverly he had pulled me back into the scenario.

I said, "But I've already told you all I can about the Dean's office and what I saw."

"But you and the Dean's secretary together might see the *importance* of something that otherwise might be overlooked."

What could I say? Even as he spoke, he was leading us down the hallway to the Dean's office. I thought about stopping and hurrying into the ladies room, but I had the distinct impression that he would be waiting when I came out. So I gave up and marched alongside Nora.

The two policemen in the office looked busy and efficient. One was snapping pictures, the other was dusting for fingerprints. The duster looked up and said, "Morning, Jake."

Fleshman said, "How's it going? About through?"

"Yeah. Got too many fingerprints. Looks like Grand Central Station. And I had to chase that cowboy out of here."

"Who?"

"The guy with the cowboy hat and boots. Name's Clyde or Clancy or something like that. I had to run him off."

I chimed in, my voice edged with anger. "His name is Clarence and he is our custodian." I was thinking that this policeman had an attitude problem. I didn't like either his tone or his belittling of Clarence.

"What happened?" asked Fleshman.

"He was in here, wiping the desks and picking up papers. When I told him to stop, he just looked at me like a dumb hoot-owl and kept right on. I had to manhandle him out."

My voice was sharp and I said, "That's what he *does*, officer. He's paid to wipe desks and pick up papers and take care of our offices. That's what the word *custodian* means."

Fleshman shot a glance at me, and I stared right back at him. The policeman's face turned red, and he sputtered, "Looked like he was getting rid of evidence. If you ask me, he is probably the one who offed the guy. He's got arms like an ape."

"You idiot," I said.

Fleshman interrupted, He said, "It's okay, Officer, "You did your job. I'll take care of Clarence." The photographer, who had retreated behind the Dean's desk, said, "I'm finished in here."

Fleshman waited until the two men left, then said to me in a firm voice, "I *will* talk to Clarence. Along with everybody else, he's a suspect, and he will be until I'm sure he's innocent."

"Clarence was simply *here* when it happened, as I was."

"I know that. And I need to talk to you two together and at length about what you saw."

I had pushed him enough. I shut up. He motioned Nora and me into the Dean's office. I stood aside to let her go in first. I knew the body was gone, but I had seen a lot of T.V. murder mysteries in my time, and I expected to see a dark outline of the Dean's body traced on the rug.

I was wrong. And relieved. Papers and files were still scattered everywhere, and the cabinets remained open. It was a mess, as Nora had said.

Fleshman asked, "Do either of you see anything unusual? Or anything missing?"

I wondered why he would think we could see anything but a totally wrecked office with papers and files scattered all over. But I looked around again to please him. Nora was looking carefully, and in a minute she said, "The Dean kept a locked strongbox in his credenza. I don't see it."

Fleshman said, "What was in it?".

"I don't know," she said, shrugging. "Personal documents, I suppose.

He turned to me. "Do you see anything unusual, Dr. Crashaw?"

"No." Then I paused a brief second, and added, "Why would anyone grind the chrysanthemums into the carpet?"

Fleshman shrugged and said, "I don't know. It probably happened in the struggle."

"I don't think so. They would have been scattered everywhere. Someone terribly angry must have thrown them down and then ground them into this one spot."

He was looking intently at me, and I was suddenly very self-conscious. He said, "Hum, that's interesting, I'll think about it."

We broke eye contact and he turned to Nora. He said, "When did you last see Dean Stafford?"

"Friday afternoon, about 5:30 p.m. I had compiled the spring schedules from the various departments and made up a master copy for the Dean. I put the schedules on his desk for him to check. He had a lot of other paperwork to do, but he told me I could go."

"Did he seem to be overly concerned about anything?, Or nervous? Anything different about him? Did he have a appointment with someone for Sunday evening?"

"No. He seemed fine when I left, and as far as I know he didn't have an appointment."

"Does the Dean work often at night?"

"Yes. Working at night, even Sunday, was not unusual for him." She made it sound as if the Dean were a conscientious, over-worked administrator who was plagued by inefficient chairpersons.

I couldn't resist. I said, "He works at night because he's never in his office before noon on work days."

It was the truth, of course, but it sounded hateful and petty when I said it. But at this point, I really didn't care. I was tired and weary of the whole thing.

I turned to Fleshman and added, "And if you don't mind, Detective, I'd like to leave, I've told you everything I know." I started toward the door.

"But I do mind, Dr. Crashaw." The tone of his voice stopped me in my tracks. Annoyed, I turned around. A faint smile creased his face, "I might need your advice."

I thought about stalking right on out the door, but a warning voice went off in my head telling me that the smart thing was to sit back down.

He moved over to the Dean's desk and leaned against it, motioning Nora and me to take empty chairs directly in front of him. He had both of us in his direct view. He looked at Nora and said, "Has the Dean had any serious problems with anyone lately? An angry student? An upset professor? A disgruntled staff member?"

She glanced at me before she said, "Three weeks ago the Dean called two of the English professors into his office. They were in trouble."

She cut her eyes toward me. "I'd say those were serious problems, wouldn't you, Dr. Crashaw?"

I knew what she was talking about and I could do nothing but nod my head in agreement. She was referring to a meeting I previously had with Chris Herndon and Eddie Parsons and the Dean. My stomach began to churn. Just remembering the meeting caused the bile to burn in my stomach.

Herndon was our resident drunk who very craftily managed to stay comfortably high twenty-four hours a day. His coffee cup was always filled with vodka, and he was such a long time drunk that he never stumbled as he walked. But his discussions in class were sometimes just chatty garbage, or a wandering and essentially a meaningless analysis of an obscure poet. Some students complained, but most of them took the easy A or B he gave the class, and laughed behind his back. .

Parsons thought of himself as an incarnate Lothario whose sole purpose in life was to seduce as many women as possible.

His technique was subtle and cunning. He read the Romantic poets and feigned a mysterious and romantic background of a heart-broken and disillusioned older man who had lost his Beloved. This act appealed to some of the younger, and less wise, students who much later found out that, in fact, he was only "a dirty old man."

Both men had been extremely successful in achieving their unsavory goals, and they had bonded together with a strange brotherhood that made them lie and cover for each other.

Fleshman looked at me. "What happened?"

I decided I would be brief and honest. "Dr. Herndon had been accused by several students of being drunk and insulting in class. The Dean questioned him, he denied that it happened. The Dean put a written reprimand in his file."

I didn't look at Nora, who had heard the heated argument. If she wanted to tell Fleshman that a furious Herndon had said to the Dean "I'll see you in hell for *that* reprimand," she could.

"And the other professor?"

Again, I kept my response simple. "Dr. Parsons had been called in because of a sexual harassment complaint. The Dean showed him the condemning letter from the student. Parsons whipped out letters from three other female students in the class who stated that Parson's accuser was at fault. *She* had been the aggressor. When Parsons spurned her, she had vowed to get him."

"How did the Dean react?"

"He was very angry. He told Parsons that he would not stand for those kinds of actions and that one day he would have enough evidence to get him fired.

"What did Parsons say?"

He said, "You'll have to do better than get a love-sick student to accuse me, Dean. And unless you have substantial evidence, don't call me in again."

I remembered the insolent smirk Parsons had given the Dean. It was as if he were daring the Dean to do something.

I said, "That made Dean Stafford furious."

The Detective's voice was quizzical as he said, "Why would the Dean take this abuse? Why didn't he just fire them on the spot?"

This time I smiled at him. "Both are tenured, full professors. To get rid of a tenured full professor is as difficult as keeping an ice cube from melting in hell.   It's practically impossible."

"I see," he said. "Then I'll talk to them." He looked at Nora and said, "Anything else?"

"Yes," she said. "One more thing. The Dean bought an insurance policy some time ago, and trusted me to keep it for him. I have it in my safe at home. .He told me the amount of it and who his beneficiary is when he gave it to me for safe-keeping.

I think you need to know the amount and the beneficiary. It pays five hundred thousand dollars and the beneficiary is Helen Stafford, his ex-wife."

Chapter 6

Fleshman had ended the meeting shortly after that statement. I think he wanted to be certain that what Nora had said was correct. Or maybe he wanted more time to check carefully on Parsons and Herndon. I was glad that this meeting was over..

As everyone began to leave, I loaded my books, and hurried out to my car. As I guided the Honda carefully through the traffic on my way home, I turned over in my mind again and again the shocking news that the Dean had made Helen his beneficiary in his life insurance. Why in the world would he do that? The premiums must have been enormous. Had something happened that made him think they might get back together?

I shook my head, perplexed. It didn't make sense. Then another scary thought popped into my mind. Would that much money have motivated Helen to kill the Dean? I couldn't imagine that scenario, but Fleshman's interest had picked up at the news.

Fleshman would certainly be checking Helen's alibi again. If Helen had stashed a young man upstairs the night of the Dean's death, surely now she would bring the young lover in so that he could speak up. He would be her alibi. It was an interesting dilemma, and I would not want to be in Helen's shoes.

I slowed the car down as I turned into my neighborhood. The night was dark and I was glad to see the street lights on. I spied Aunt Grace's '65 Mustang convertible parked in the driveway. I sighed. She had warned me not to drive the short distance to the University and now she had driven from across town to see me. Once inside the garage I struggled with my heavy briefcase, banging it against my knees a couple of times before I got the kitchen door open and scurried inside. Aunt Grace was seated at the small table, her hands wrapped around a tea cup, a broad smile on her face. I dropped my briefcase and gloves on the counter and blew on my cold hands. "What are you doing here, Aunt Grace?"

"I'm glad to see you too, Constance. Would you like a cup of tea?" Her eyes sparkled with energy.

"Sure," I said, sighing and looking around for Tess. She was usually underfoot, rubbing my legs, wanting attention by the time I opened the door.

I asked again, "What are you doing out in this weather, Aunt Grace?" As she often does, Aunt Grace ignored my question completely. She said, "Tell me what happened that night. Were you scared to death? Was it awful?"

"Where is Tess?"

She squirmed and said, "I don't know. When she saw me, she tore out of the room.

I replied as calmly as I could, "Where she no doubt climbed to the top of the highest bookcase."

"Constance, will you stop yammering about that infernal cat and talk to me about what happened?"

I poured a cup of tea and sat down across from her. "The Dean was murdered." The pungent odor of the herbal tea was pleasant. I took a sip.

She tapped her fingers on the table. "I know *that*. But what did you do, when you found him, I mean? Were you there alone.? Her voice trailed off.

I relented. She was not just being curious. She was worried and frightened. I placed my hand over hers. "Clarence was there too. He came in the office right after I found the Dean."

"That must have been a shock, finding the Dean like that."

"Yes." I pulled my hand away from her.
I didn't want her to feel it tremble.

"Did you see anyone? Hear anything?"

"No, I didn't see anyone." I paused. "I heard the sound of the argument, and I heard footsteps afterwards. That's all. So don't fret, the murderer has no reason to be afraid of me."

"But you were there. That makes me very nervous."

I smiled. "Do you still think I should help solve the murder?"

She ignored my question. "This Jacob Fleshman, how long has he been on the police force? Does he have a good record?

"I don't know how long he has been in the department, but he is very sharp."

Her bright blue eyes were in their speculative mode. She had more questions to ask, and the simplest course was to let her talk. "Did the detective find any clues?"

I didn't want to tell her about the condoms or describe the wrecked office in any detail. "I suppose everything in the Dean's office is a potential clue."

"Do you have any cookies?" Her quick jump from one subject to another was typical Aunt Grace, and I had learned not to be surprised by it. I rummaged around, found a box of Oreos, and set a plateful on the table. "What are you thinking, Aunt Grace?"

"Someone from the University did it," she said. Her statement was unequivocal.

"Why do you say that? It could have been an outsider."

"No. It had to be someone who hated the Dean, knew his routine, had the opportunity."

I interrupted. "Not to mention the ability to use a heavy something, probably a statue, to kill him." Again I saw the Dean's crushed head, saw his twisted leg, smelled the blood. And the thought flashed through my mind that it had to have been someone very strong and very angry to have done that. I gulped the hot tea.

She said, "It makes sense, Constance. You've said the Dean had terrible fights with you, with several professors in your department, with others in Liberal Arts. No doubt some of the Administrators had tangled with him as well."

What she was saying made sense, and if she were right that meant that someone I knew had killed Dean Stafford.

She said what I was thinking. "That's very frightening. What are you going to do?"

"I'll cooperate with the detective, help him any way I can. You're not to worry."

"You're like your mother, Constance. Willful, stubborn, but you've got courage." I wondered where that accolade came from, but I didn't reply. Instead, I looked at the kitchen clock and saw that it was eleven o'clock already. I was frazzled, and I assumed Aunt Grace was spending the night with me. So I said, "If you're through with your tea and cookies, I'll get your bed ready."

"No need," she said. "I'm going home."

"Look at the time, Aunt Grace. It's too late and the roads are dangerous."

She raised an imperious hand. "No offense, Constance, but I sleep better in my own bed. The streets will be clear of traffic, and I'll zip right over to my house." She was gathering up her coat and purse as she spoke.

"That convertible isn't heavy enough to keep you from spinning if you hit a patch of ice."

"I won't spin. It will take me forty-five minutes to get across town, I'll call you."

"Aunt Grace," I began.

"Don't forget our luncheon date for Wednesday. And tell that detective to concentrate on University people if he wants to find the murderer in a hurry." She paused at the door and added "You are bright and inquisitive, Constance, and you can help."

"Aunt Grace," I said, but I was talking to the cold draught of wind that blew in behind her. I listened until I heard the roar of her motor, and I watched the car until I saw the taillights disappear around the corner. I wanted to shake her, but I had to admire her independence. I put the cups and plates into the dishwasher and flipped out the kitchen lights.

Through the windows I could see the snow that had drifted over the deck, marking it as a smooth white rectangle. The bushes that lined the back fence huddled together like white-sheeted dwarfs trying to keep from freezing.

I walked into the den to rescue Tess. I stood just inside the doorway and saw her perched on the bookcase. I said, "It's okay, Tess, you can come down. Aunt Grace is gone." Tess is smart and she understands English better than many of my students. She stretched luxuriously, arched her back gracefully and then jumped down at my feet. Without waiting for me, she darted ahead toward the bedroom.

I stepped into the den to turn off the lights but the flames in the fireplace looked so warm and comforting, I slouched down in a chair for a moment. I hadn't liked Dean Stafford, but he didn't deserve to die as he had. I was going to help Detective Fleshman if I could. How could I help him?" I went back over Sunday evening, keeping my mind as clear and focused as I could. Was there anything, however slight, that I had missed?

It was so quiet I could hear the wind whispering around the corners of the house. I was mesmerized by the fireplace flames, but nothing came to mind. I sighed, pushed out of the chair. I thought, "Maybe tomorrow when my mind is fresher I can think of something"

I walked out into the hallway, and glanced into my small office. The computer was blinking that I had e-mail. I walked into the room, stretched my back and flexed my shoulder muscles to ease the tightness at the base of my neck. I yawned, and hit the key to retrieve the message. My yawn stopped in mid-air so abruptly that I felt my jaw crack. Staring at me in bold black letters was a message.

THE DEAN WAS A PERVERT. HE GOT WHAT HE DESERVED.   KEEP YOUR DAMN MOUTH SHUT. OR ELSE.

Chapter 7

I stood very still, eyeing the computer for another second. Then I automatically reached for the mouse and hit print. I sat down while the brief message clacked out and I read it again. The words looked very official, like a bureaucratic memo sent out to scare a low level employee into action.

My first thought was that it was from an irate student wanting to get even for an F grade. I balled it up and threw it toward the trash can. But I didn't move, I sat there a minute longer. Then I picked up the note, smoothed it out, and read it again. Not a student.

It *was* something Boyd Finnell, in a fit of pique, might have written. But that was my prejudice speaking. I had to admit it could be a serious threat, not just a spiteful retaliation for an imagined wrong or a petty attempt to harass me.

That was even more frightening. I stuck the note in my pocket, walked quickly down the hall to the kitchen, checked to see if the door that led into the garage was locked. I thought about the door off the kitchen to the patio. I sometimes forgot to lock it. I turned off the lights in the kitchen so the curtainless windows wouldn't frame me in light. I rattled the patio door. It was latched.

The French door in the small bedroom! It had only a push button lock. I ran down the hall past the office, into the room, and flipped on the light. The button was pushed in. The door was locked.

Anger at the whole thing was beginning to replace my fear, and I grabbed the phone, thinking that I would call Fleshman. Then I glanced at my watch. It was twelve thirty, not a good time to call him. But I could dial Matt and I did.

His phone rang five times before he answered. His voice was husky with sleep and his "hello" was not particularly cheery.

I said, "It's me." I could imagine him yawning and rubbing his face to wake up enough to ask why I had called in the middle of the night. I took the initiative. "I know it's late, but I got the damndest message on my PC."

"Yeah," he said not very enthusiastically, "What?"

"It's a warning, maybe a threat. It says the Dean got what he deserved, and I better keep my mouth shut."

His voice lost its sleepiness. "Are you alone?"

"Well, of course. What's that got to do. . .?"

He stopped me. "I'll be there in twenty minutes."

I remembered the icy streets, and I began to feel a little foolish. "Hey, wait, it's probably just a crank note. A bummed out student, or more likely, one of the profs who didn't like his fall schedule." I managed a laugh. "Besides, you might wreck your Jag, the streets are slick."

"If I do, I'll buy another one," he said and the line went dead.

I looked at the phone, slipped it back on its cradle, glad he was coming over. I thought about brewing coffee, but I didn't want to go back to the kitchen. If someone happened to be lurking outside, the uncurtained windows made it easy to see everything.

I walked into the den and began pacing in front of the fireplace, imagining how Matt would speed over. Thinking about his confident "I'll buy another Jag if I wreck this one," I had to smile. He had offered to buy me a Jaguar when Eric had tossed me aside. He had said. "It'll help your ego and your image,"

He would have done it had I not stopped him. He was very wealthy, having inherited a large fortune from his parents, and he was very generous toward me.

As I waited, I took several deep breaths to make me relax and then I sat back down on the couch. The flames in the fireplace danced in the darkness, pushing back the shadows. It was quiet; I could hear the clock on the mantle ticking off the minutes.

Fifteen minutes later, Matt was pounding on the front door. I unlocked the door, and he shrugged out of his coat, dropped it to the floor and pulled me up against him.

"Are you okay?" he asked.

I didn't want to say anything; I just wanted him to hold me. The warmth of his breath on my face, the roughness of his cheek against mine, the lingering fragrance of his after shave lotion, were very comforting.

Finally, I pulled back, and saw the concern in his eyes. I said, "You could say I'm a little shook up, but I'm okay."

"You're sure?"

"Yes." My voice was shaky.

He said, "Let me see the note." I handed it to him and he sat down by the kitchen table, I sat on a chair across from him. "What do you think, Matt?"

"I don't know. It could be a disgruntled student, or some sick wacko getting his kicks. Or maybe one of your distinguished English professors. They're a quirky lot."

I knew that he was trying to make me feel better, keep me from being scared. I waited a long minute before I asked the question uppermost in my mind.

"Could it be the murderer?"

He handed me the note. "I don't think so, it would be too risky."

"I'll tell Fleshman about it."

"Sure, that's his business."

Just having him sitting there made me feel safe. I said, "Want a cup of coffee?"

He grinned. "I'll help you make it."

I turned on all the lights in the hallway and flipped on the patio lights. With Matt beside me, the darkness didn't seem so formidable.

I filled my old coffee maker and it began its usual hissing and sputtering, reminding me that I needed to buy a new one. It finally hiccuped its last drop and I filled a mug, took a tentative sip to see if it was drinkable, and handed it to Matt. He took a deep swallow, grinned, and said, "That's graduate school coffee. Guaranteed to keep you awake all night." His voice sobered. "The note scared you."

"Sure as hell did. "Finding the Dean lying in a pool of blood scared me. I'm feeling pretty vulnerable, Matt."

He reached out, took my hand and pulled me down beside him again. He said, I understand, but let's look logically at what's happened."

"Like a philosophy professor, you mean?"

He laughed. "That's right. From the viewpoint of a logical philosophy professor, which I just happen to be. First, I don't think that you need to be afraid. You really didn't see anything."

"But. Matt . . . ."

He shushed me. "Think, Con. You happened to be at the university at the wrong time. You found the Dean, but you didn't see the murderer, did you?"

I said, "No." He was correct, of course, but I was still jittery. I asked, "Then why the note?"

He said, "Maybe just an angry student? Or just someone intent on upsetting you? Or some sick idiot wanting to exploit a murder?"

"So you're saying what?"

"Let the cops handle it. Fleshman seems competent enough."

I sighed. He was right, Fleshman could handle it. I said, "Okay."

He smiled. "Okay. Now if you'll get me another cup of that terrible coffee, I'll tell you about my trip to Holyoke to see Annette."

He wanted to change the subject and that was fine with me. I'd be glad to put both the e mail and the murder out of my mind while I heard about his daughter Annette, one of my favorite people. I poured a fresh cup from the carafe and said, "How is Annette?"

He looked pleased. He said, "She's good. She is happy to be doing her senior year at Holyoke."

"It must be quite a change from her first year at Harding?"

He took a sip of coffee. "The course work is tougher, but the teachers are special. Lots of tutorials."

"Too bad she couldn't make it home for Christmas."

"Yeah. It just wasn't convenient." He stood up. "Let's go and enjoy the fireplace."

I snapped off lights and followed him. He settled on the couch, and I slouched down in my oversized recliner. We were both quiet, and it was peaceful. I watched the light from the fireplace soften the planes of his face, glance off his rumpled

44

hair. He *was* good-looking.

He saw me watching him and his face crinkled into a smile, chasing the shadows away. "Want me to stay the night?"

I laughed, remembering the nights he had stayed. After Eric, he had spent many nights with me just as a friend. Then one night he had stayed and we had become lovers. It was a sweet and healing time and had lasted for six months.

I said, "I hoped you would."

He was remembering also. He said, "You should have married me then, Con."

"I was too battered and bruised, feeling too betrayed. It wouldn't have worked."

He smiled. "The offer still stands."

I reached for his hand. "Come on, I'll get you a toothbrush. I don't have any pajamas that'll fit.

"Doesn't matter." He grinned. "I still sleep in my boxers. Most of the time."

In spite of myself, I blushed. "You can sleep in the back bedroom."

He laughed. "Right next to yours?"

"That's right," I said, gathering up Tess who had fallen asleep in a chair. She raised her head, but quickly flopped it back on my arm.

He said, "If you won't marry me, I've got a second proposal. Tomorrow let's hop in my plane and fly to San Diego. Get some rays and thaw out. Take in a little night life. Or, if you'd rather, we'll fly up to San Francisco for the opera. It'll be my treat."

"I'd love to, Matt, but you know we can't. The Dean's funeral is tomorrow. You know we will have to attend."

He groaned. "Damn it, I don't want to attend the Dean's funeral. I want to get out of this deep freeze we're in. I want to run on the beach, dance the night away." He paused. "It would be great fun."

"No argument with that. But we've got two and a half weeks before classes begin. We'll go. Later. I promise."

"Okay." His smile was rueful, but he leaned over, pushed my hair back from my face, and gave me a brief kiss. "Sleep well," he said.

I plodded wearily to my bedroom, put Tess in her favorite

sleeping spot, the window seat, and turned off the lamp. Pushing my tired body under the comforter, I thought I would fall instantly asleep.

It didn't happen. Matt's proposal had stirred up memories, memories I thought lay buried in the mist of the past. Memories of Eric, of our consuming passion for each other for the first two years of our marriage, flooded over me. I tried to push the feelings away but it was useless. I tried not to remember the day he told me the fire was gone, and he wanted out, but the pain was back, sharp and painful as it had ever been.

Would I ever forget? I got up and opened the drapes. I looked outside. The moon, round and full, was a huge spotlight showcasing the snow packed landscape. The trees, powdered with heavy snow, and the ground, pristine white in the moonlight, looked picture-card perfect. It looked like a fairyland, but I shivered and closed the drapes tightly.

It was *not* a fairyland. It was a real world where love died, and some hurts never healed. It was a nightmare world where murderers roamed and perverts preyed on the helpless. No one was really safe. The wind whipped through the trees, the snow swirled and tapped against the draped window.

And I was still afraid.

Chapter 8

I had no choice but to go to the Dean's funeral on Friday. I had a memo on my desk from Vice President Munsell notifying me that he expected me to be there. His arrogance in making such a demand did not surprise me. It was a typical act of an egocentric bureaucrat who found delight in throwing his weight around.

I would have gone to the Dean's funeral of course, out of some confused sense of doing the appropriate thing. He had been my boss, and there had been a few times when he had helped resolve problems with difficult students. The least I could do was to attend his funeral and show a modicum of respect for him. It seemed to me that he deserved that much, no matter how shabbily and shoddily I thought he had lived his life.

Matt finally agreed to go with me, but I had had to use all my persuasive powers on him. He didn't want to go. He thought it hypocritical to pretend to grieve over someone you didn't even like. I didn't argue with him over that point. Instead I appealed to his sympathy by telling him that I had not been to a funeral since my mother died, and I was very nervous about going to this one alone. That's what finally swung him over.

He picked me up at the University and we drove through the outer edges of Warwick Hills, the wealthy and exclusive section of Oklahoma City, to Saint Martin's Episcopal Church where the services were to be held. Matt wasn't saying much, so I broke the silence by asking, "Why haven't you moved to Warwick Hills, Matt? It's where the rich and famous live."

"I'm one of the rich and famous?"

"Well, one of the rich. Wouldn't you like to hobnob with the movers-and-shakers of the City and their beautiful women?"

"Not my cup of tea."

I sighed. "Mixing and mingling with them was very important to Dean Stafford."

He didn't respond, but it didn't matter. We had arrived at the church. Saint Martins was a monolithic structure of red brick, with a steeple that split the blue sky and towered into the clouds. Its bells, magnificent and powerful, could be heard in the downtown streets of Oklahoma City, several blocks away. The church reflected the affluence of the area and the opulence of its parishioners.

We were early. Only a few other people had arrived, and they were sitting near the front. I didn't recognize any of them and I wondered if they were distant relatives of the Dean, or out-of-town friends. I looked around. None of the rich and beautiful crowd had arrived. I wondered if any of his society friends from the City itself would bother to come.

Matt guided me toward a pew near the back. I was glad, I had no desire to be any closer. Our footsteps were soundless on the heavy plush carpet. We sank quietly onto the heavily cushioned mahogany pews. In spite of lights gleaming along the walls, the interior was somber and dark. Even the magnificent stained glass windows, which must have reflected lavish color and warmth on a sunshiny day, were dull and muted.

"Very impressive," I whispered to Matt. He nodded.

The organist made her entrance, sat down, arranged the music and began to play softly. Ten minutes later there was a slight stir as a group entered together. They sat down two rows from us, obviously nervous and ill at ease.

I recognized two of the women from their pictures in the society section of the Daily Oklahoman. One of them was prominent in Republican circles and the other one, if I remembered correctly, worked for the cause of Aids.

I whispered, "Some of the Dean's society friends made it." Matt glanced at them, but didn't respond.

"Not many here from Liberal Arts." I said. Matt touched my hand briefly, a signal to be quiet, I supposed. I straightened up and locked my hands together in my lap, determined to sit quietly and wait until after the service to talk to Matt about who or who wasn't here.

Then suddenly, a morbid thought flashed into my mind.

I thought, "How many people would crowd the church to attend my funeral? Any more than were coming to pay their respects to the Dean?"

That was such an uncomfortable thought that I shut my eyes, determined to pray that I would be less abrasive and more congenial with people I had to deal with day after day.

When I opened my eyes, Vice President Munsell, followed by Lew Hawkins, was making his way toward the front. I wondered if he was going to have some part in the service.

Trying to be unobtrusive, I glanced around one more time to see if Nora Tennyson had come in. She had. She was sitting on the very back row, and I saw Boyd Finnell taking a seat alongside her.

I had expected Nora, but Finnell surprised me. I was sure he hadn't come out of any sense of sorrow over the Dean's death. More than likely he wanted to see who was there so he could gossip about it all over campus.

The organ continued to play. Then the side door opened and Helen Stafford, beautiful in black, walked in on the arm of a young man. They sat down in the front row with the young man looking very uncomfortable by her side. She carefully wiped away a tear, and I found myself wondering if it was a tear of grief over the Dean's death, or a tear of joy at being the recipient of a half million dollars.

The ritual of the Episcopal faith was long and elaborate, and, as most reminders of human frailty are, disturbing. I found myself wishing that my own faith in things religious was stronger.

I was relieved when the service finally ended. Matt and I were two of the first out of the sanctuary. I didn't wait to speak to anyone; I wanted to go somewhere lively and have a stiff drink. We hurried across the parking lot toward Matt's car. The sun was sinking behind heavy dark clouds, and a cold wind whipped snow around our feet. I shivered and sank deeper into my coat. I said, "Let's get out of here, Matt, I need a stiff bourbon."

But before I could get into the car, Munsell, who was just behind us, called out, "Wait up, Dr. Crashaw." He was puffing and his face was pink from cold and exertion. He is shorter than I am by several inches, and I could see the bald spot on his head gleaming in the fading light.

He caught up with us and said, "You *are* going to the cemetery." It was another command, not a question or a request.

A trip to the cemetery was the last thing I had in mind. I had fulfilled my obligation, if I had one, to the Dean's memory by attending the funeral. But his remark caught me by surprise, and threw me off stride. I stammered, "I don't know. . . ."

He said, "I'd like for you to ride along with me, if you will." He managed a thin smile, but it was all surface, with no warmth. My first impulse was to say no, but I caught myself up short. He was the Vice President, and he was my superior in the area of Administration. It would be wise to keep in his good graces. Surely the ceremony at the cemetery would be short. I could meet Matt later.

I said, "Well, yes, I can."

Matt, who had been waiting, smiled and said, "Then I'll see you later, Connie." He headed toward his own car.

Munsell and I walked, both silent, toward his car. It was not until he had moved into line with the small group of cars heading for the cemetery that he said anything. Then it was a platitude, "It was a nice service."

It was an awkward moment. I said, "Yes, it was." I hadn't the slightest idea why he had asked me to ride with him, so I stared straight ahead as if keeping the tail lights of the car in front of us was vitally important.

We wound our way back through Warwick Hills, speeding up when we reached the main highway heading north. The street lights had come on, but they did little to dispel the encroaching darkness.

We had ridden a mile or so in the funeral procession before Munsell spoke again. He cleared his throat and said, "Ah, I guess the Dean's office; that is, his papers, have all been put back in some kind of order?"

I hadn't expected a question about the Dean's files, and it took me a second to respond. He had been in the Dean's office several times since the Dean's death, much to Nora's irritation, checking on what was going on. He certainly knew the progress that Nora had made.

I said, "Ms. Tennyson has been working very hard to get things back in order."

He said, a slight smile on his face, "It's very important that everything be back in its proper place with the files ready for the next Dean, you know."

Was this my cue to tell him I wanted to be considered for the position of the new dean? I thought about it for a second and decided that even if it were, I was not going to pick up on his innuendo. Much as I wanted the deanship, it seemed crass and inappropriate to be politicking for the job of the man whose funeral we had just attended. I said, "I'm sure that the records will be ready in good time."

"Yes," he said, "Well, that's all very well," and paused.

I had the feeling that he had not yet asked the question that he wanted to ask . I waited.

"Do you have any of the Dean's records, or special files, in your office?"

I was glad it was dark and he couldn't see the surprise on my face. *What in hell was he getting at?*

I said, "No, of course not. Why would I?"

He turned and looked at me for what seemed a long minute and said, "When I talked with the Dean just a few days before his untimely death, he gave me the distinct impression that he, ah, had trusted some sensitive files into your keeping."

I was dumbfounded. Not only had the Dean never given me any of *his* files, he had insisted that all pertinent personnel files of the English faculty be kept in his office.

What was bothering this man? What was he talking about? I hadn't a clue. Attempting to be both respectful and at the same time honest, I said, "I'm sorry, but no, the Dean didn't leave any files with me."

My answer had not pleased him, and I had the uneasy notion that he thought I was not telling the truth. He frowned and stared straight ahead, and I braced myself for another question. But he didn't say anything more.

The silence between us lengthened and became oppressive. I tried to think of something to say that would be innocuous and disarming, but I couldn't. I sat stony still beside him.

When we approached the burial grounds at the small cemetery, he said, "I'll need to fill the vacancy left by Dean Stafford soon, and your name is in consideration. I need someone who will work closely with me. Someone in whom I have complete confidence, and whose loyalty is unquestioned."

I had the distinct feeling that I was being tested, and that my answer was important. I chose my words carefully, but I was determined to be honest.

I said, "I appreciate your consideration." I paused a second and added, "I can promise you that I would be a diligent and hard-working dean, that I would do whatever I could to promote the University."

His answer was an enigmatic, "I see." His pale eyes were cool and aloof.

I had no idea if I had passed the test or not. We got out of his car and made our way to the burial site.

Only a handful of people stood near the open grave. It was Helen Stafford and her young man, Nora Tennyson and a trio of the well-dressed society women and their escorts, and a few late-arriving stragglers.

The larger group at the church had melted away and not come for the burial service. We all looked cold and uncomfortable and anxious to get away. The minister was merciful. He read a few verses of scripture and prayed a short dismissal prayer.

I pulled my collar up and turned to go, hoping that the ride back to the University would be silent and quick. It was then that I saw Detective Fleshman standing several feet away.

"Hello, Dr. Crashaw," he said. He wore a navy blue double breasted overcoat, gloves and a scarf, but his head was bare and his dark hair was ruffled by the sharp wind. He looked handsome. I was glad to see him. I said, "Hello, Detective."

"Can I give you a ride home? I'd like to talk over a few things with you. If that's convenient, I mean?" I jumped at the chance to get away from Munsell. I had no desire to field any more of his questions.

I said to Munsell "I guess I should do as the detective asks, then added, "Thank you for bringing me."

"Of course," He smiled at Fleshman, tipped his hat, and said, "Good evening, Detective."

We watched as he waddled away. Then we turned and headed for Fleshman's car. I jumped in. "You saved my life," I said, as I settled into the seat. "I couldn't have borne another thirty minutes with Munsell."

He smiled. "That bad, huh?"

"Terrible. He is not what you'd call a charming man, and he kept asking me if I had any of the Dean's files. He thought the Dean might have left a personal file of some kind with me."

"Did he? Leave anything with you, I mean?"

I laughed. "You don't know how protective and secretive the Dean was about anything that concerned him. I'd be the last person he would confide in."

Sleet, mingled with snow, was hitting the windshield. It had been a bad day for a funeral. I said, "I was surprised to see you." He smiled faintly. "Sometimes the murderer shows up at his victim's funeral." The thought chilled me. How could anyone be that cold-blooded? I said, "Why in the world would he do that?"

"I don't know. Maybe because his absence would be too conspicuous? Maybe to gloat over killing him? People do strange things for strange reasons, Dr. Crashaw."

"Do you think he was there?"

"I don't know," he said. "The crowd was small."

"Not as many as the Dean would have wanted, I'm sure."

He said, "I came for another reason as well. I'd like to talk to you and Clarence together tomorrow. Can I meet you at the University, say around ten o'clock?"

"That's fine for me. I can contact Clarence"

"When I talked to Clarence the other day, he told me that 'he saw a tall sailor' that night, but he wouldn't, or couldn't, elaborate, on that. I thought that maybe you could help me find out what he's talking about."

"Maybe," I said. "I'm not sure I always understand what is on his mind. But Clarence and I are friends, I'll try.

"Good," he said.

I leaned back against the cushions. I was getting a dull headache and I was also getting depressed. It had not been a good day. But I had no premonition that the next day would be worse.

Actually, one of the worst days in my life.

Chapter 9

The phone was ringing. Groggy, I reached for it, knocked the base to the floor and juggled the receiver. I glared at the bedside clock. It was 6:35 a.m. Who could be calling this early in the morning? My hello was not cordial.

"I won't take this damn spring schedule. Eighteenth century poetry and three composition classes? That's not going to happen. I told you I wanted a course in Twain, which you ignored completely. You didn't give anybody else a schedule as tough as this."

It was Finnell. Damn him. "Slow down, Dr. Finnell," I said, trying to get my wits together. I had put the spring schedules in the mail boxes late yesterday afternoon. He must have been hanging around all day, waiting for a chance to find something he could use to challenge me.

I should have known he would be on my back. The only way to placate him was to let him set up his own schedule, and this time I had deliberately not done so. I didn't think he deserved any special consideration, and more than that, I was fed up with his griping.

"I'm not going to sign off on this schedule." His voice was adamant.

"Then don't. I don't give a damn. And stop calling me at home. I don't work on Saturdays."

"You don't seem to be working much on any day. And since you are seldom in your office, where you should be, I'll call you whenever I want to."

"You are completely out of line, Dr. Finnell. If you have any further complaints, see me on Monday."

I was furious. I grabbed up the phone to slam the receiver in his ear.

He hissed, "Guess you're too busy with the Detective to take care of your job."

"What?"

"I saw you at the cemetery after the funeral, talking to him. You two looked very cozy."

I couldn't believe his arrogance, his stupidity. I hissed back, "You go to hell, Finnell," and slammed the receiver down as hard as I could. I hoped it would shatter his eardrums.

Shoving the blankets back, I swung my legs off the side of the bed and looked out the window, trying to calm down.

Why did I let such a miserable, hateful, conniving idiot upset me? Because he was all of those things and more, and I was powerless to do anything but listen to his tirades. Damn tenure, damn his political connections.

I was beginning to get a caffeine-deprived headache, I shoved my reluctant body off the bed and padded down the hall to the kitchen.

I put the coffee on to brew and looked around for Tess. She had been meowing earlier, but I had ignored her. She was nowhere in sight. I hurried outside to pick up the newspaper and glanced at the heavy gray clouds. They were fat with either sleet or snow, and we were in for more cold weather. I shivered my way back into the warm kitchen.

Tess had come out of hiding and was lying on the top of the double oven, her favorite place. It was warm and comfortable and a strategic spot from to launch an attack. She eyed me briefly, then, a limp, ragdoll of a cat, dropped her head between her front paws and flattened out.

The coffee pot sputtered, coughed, and finally stopped. I poured myself a cup of the muddy-looking brew, and took a cautious sip. It was okay. Strong and pungent, good enough to jump-start me. I swigged it down, then stood up and forced myself into a series of stretches and squats and kicks that made me feel a little more lively.

I heaved a sigh, glanced at the clock. I had plenty of time. My meeting with Fleshman and Clarence was at ten. I poured another cup of coffee.

Forty minutes later I was pulling into the parking lot at the LA Building. Several cars were parked there and I was in a hurry. I was already ten minutes late, but I waited until the driver of a university pickup truck finished dumping sand on the icy pavement.

He motioned me into a cleared parking slot. I walked

cautiously toward the LA Building and quickly tugged open the front door, grateful for the warm air that enveloped me. *Thank God for Clarence! He got here early, found a frigid building, and turned up the thermostat.* Turning the thermostat down to a frigid 60 degrees over the weekend was a witless attempt by the administration to keep costs down.

I smiled. I halfway expected to see Clarence shuffling along in the hallway. I had called him early yesterday morning at work, and he had promised to be here.

I turned the corner and stopped in my tracks. Detective Fleshman was standing outside my office door, talking to Boyd Finnell. I said, "Good Morning, Detective Fleshman."

I looked at Finnell. "I really didn't expect to see you today, Dr. Finnell, I thought I made that clear."

His smile was fatuous, oily. He said, "Since I've been assigned the 18th century literature course, I came by to pick up the new textbook. I just happened to meet Detective Fleshman, and I was about to explain where I was on Sunday night."

Again the smile.

I had no idea what Finnell was up to, but I knew he didn't just happen to come by to pick up a book. He had an agenda.

"Then go right ahead with your alibi," I said, trying my best to make the word 'alibi' sound suspicious.

Fleshman had picked up on the tension. He said, "Will it be all right if we talked in your office, Dr. Crashaw?"

I nodded, determined that I wouldn't let Finnell rattle me. When we reached my office, I motioned them in and they sat down.

I went around the desk, took off my jacket, sat down across from them. I would keep my mouth shut and let Finnell do whatever it was he had come to do. Fleshman was no fool. He could handle him.

Hoping that Finnell would somehow get tripped up by his arrogance and his inflated sense of his self-importance, I sat back and waited

He said, "I think I have what you'd call an air-tight alibi, Detective."

Fleshman replied, "Oh. That's interesting. Not many people do."

"Well, on Sunday night I was on campus in the Field

House while the basketball final was being played. I would estimate that at least three hundred people saw me there."

"Were you with someone?"

"I sat with Alouisus Jones and Peggy Flanders."

I was not surprised. Alouisus Jones was captain of the soccer team, and one of Finnell's priorities was to cozy up to the athletes. He bragged interminably that he was the only Liberal Arts professor who supported their events.

"How long were you there?"

Finnell's face turned slightly pink, an indication that he had thought his alibi, so stated, was tight enough to satisfy Detective Fleshman.

I put my hand over my mouth to cover my smile. He had expected Fleshman to accept his alibi and his innocence without question. That wasn't going to happen.

"I was there from 7:30 until the game was over at 9:30."

"I see. And I'll be able to confirm all this when I talk to the two students?"

"Of course." Now Finnell's voice was edgy.

Better cool it, Finnell, I thought. *You're not dealing with an amateur here.* I found myself hoping that Fleshman would keep the pressure on. It was a pleasure to see Finnell squirm.

"How did you get along with the Dean? Ever have any trouble with him?" Fleshman's voice was calm and deliberative.

Finnell cut his eyes at me. *He thinks I've told Fleshman about the fights between them.* I smiled back at him.

"We had some disagreements. I didn't think he was very effective as a dean."

"Have any reason to kill him?"

Finnell's face flushed a bright red. "No, I didn't kill him. I didn't like the bastard, but I didn't kill him." The anger in his voice was palpable. "And I don't like being questioned like this."

If his plan had been to convince Fleshman of his air-tight alibi and turn attention away from himself, he was failing miserably. His famous temper and classic paranoia were making him look more and more like someone who, given the opportunity, could commit murder.

Then he said, his voice furious, "I don't like being treated like a common criminal."

He stood up and stalked toward the door. He paused.

"Check out my alibi, Detective Fleshman. You'll find it is solid as a rock."

"I will, Dr. Finnell. You'll be hearing from me."

Finnell was out the door. Fleshman smiled wryly. "You have some strange ones, Dr. Crashaw. I don't think I would want your job."

"Call me Connie. And you're right. I do have some strange ones. But I *know* I wouldn't want *your* job.

He laughed. "Not many people do -- Connie."

I liked Fleshman. He was a professional, but he was relaxed and easy to deal with. Probably because he was sure of himself.

My mind ran over all the questions that had been puzzling me about the Dean's death and I said, "Why does anyone commit a murder?"

His eyes were serious. "Why would someone kill the Dean, you mean? That's not easy to answer. It could be because of greed, or thwarted love, or someone wanting revenge. I think there are as many motives for murder as there are people."

"Then finding the motive for his murder is important, isn't it?"

"It's important. But the most important thing is to find out who had *opportunity* and *means*. Apparently, a large group of people had reason to want him dead, but not everyone had the opportunity and means. That's why I check alibis so carefully."

"So if someone doesn't have a good alibi for Sunday night that person would be a serious suspect?"

"That's right." His face was inscrutable, his eyes searching, and suddenly I was uncomfortable. I had had both opportunity and means, and I had made it pretty clear that I disliked Stafford.

I stammered, "I fit in that category."

"Yes."

"I was *there*; I had opportunity and means."

"But you didn't kill him."

I said, "No, I didn't. But the thought that I might be a suspect makes me nervous. Wouldn't the real murderer get very jittery like that at times?"

"Unless he's a stone-cold killer or a psycho, yes."

My heart sank. "And you don't think he is, do you? You think he's one of us."

His eyes were thoughtful. "I think I need to talk with you and Clarence. You were both here and together you may come up with something you hadn't thought about before. Something seemingly insignificant but which may be very important."

I relaxed a little. "He's probably in his tiny cubbyhole under the stairwell. It's the last room on the east side of the building, next to the street. If he's not busy, he slips down there to have a chew of tobacco. The Dean absolutely forbade him to chew in the halls or classrooms."

"You like Clarence, don't you?"

"He's a simple soul, and he's a good person." I smiled. "He's a kind of rare commodity around here."

We walked to the end of the hallway and I went up to the door and knocked. Fleshman looked around. "Nice place to hang out. Suits Clarence. It's off the beaten track."

I knocked again. I waited a second or two and then tried the door handle. It turned in my hand, and I pushed open the door. I said, "Clarence, it's Dr. Crashaw."

The room was dark; the blinds were still drawn. "Clarence," I said, moving into the room. Then I saw him. He was lying flat on his back on the floor beside his makeshift desk. His eyes were open and staring.

The air seemed to have been sucked out of the room, and I was having trouble breathing. I sensed that Fleshman was standing beside me. I felt his hand on my back. I said, "He's dead, isn't he?

Fleshman knelt beside Clarence, felt his throat for a pulse that wasn't there. He glanced up at me. Immediately he stood up, placing himself between Clarence and me. He took my hands in his.

"No," he said, "No, you're not going to scream, Connie. You're not."

I *was* about to. The intensity in his voice was the only thing that stopped me. I choked and gagged with the effort to swallow the scream back.

He moved quickly, turning me aside and pushing me out the door. He took my face between his hands and said, "Listen to me. I want you to go to your office, close the door, and wait there for me. Don't open the door for anyone, just wait for me." I nodded. His eyes focused on mine. "You *are* going to be all right, Connie."

I didn't think so, but the thought of being in my office, with the door locked, sounded very good at the moment. I walked down the hall slowly, my mind in a turmoil. When I got inside my office, I shut the door behind me and locked it. I slumped in my chair and held my hands together to stop their trembling. Was the whole world going mad? How could this have happened? How could Clarence be dead?

I had talked to him only yesterday morning. Our conversation ran through my mind as clearly as if I had taped it for instant replay. It had been an ordinary, no frills conversation. I had asked, "Can you meet me and the Detective, Clarence? Tomorrow? About ten? At the University?" His answer had been, "Yes, ma'am, I can."

I said, "I'm sorry to bring you back on your day off, but it's important."

"Yes, ma'am."

Grateful that he hadn't argued, I had said, "Thanks, Clarence," and started to say goodbye. Then he said, "I seen a sailor. With a big old bunched up collar," and the phone went dead. I hadn't called him back. I had thought it would be easier for him to explain what he meant if we were talking face to face.

I should have talked to him. I should have.

Fleshman tapped at the door, "It's me, Connie."

He looked at me carefully. "Are you all right?"

I managed a weak smile. "About eighty percent, I'd say." I took a deep breath. "It seems like Saturdays and Sundays are dangerous days to be on this campus."

He looked at me kindly, as if I had said something intelligent, and smiled. "They seem to be."

"Clarence is dead?"

He nodded.

"How?" I asked.

"It looks like a blow to his head, but I can't be sure until the Medical Examiner gets here."

"*Why* would anyone kill Clarence?"

"I don't know. But my best guess is that he saw something, or someone, that night."

I thought of Clarence's cryptic end to yesterday's conversation. I said, "He saw someone, I think. He mentioned to me yesterday, for the first time, that he saw a sailor."

"Did he explain what he meant?"

"No, just said he had seen one. Then he hung up the phone."

"Why would he think he had seen a sailor? There aren't any Navy men in this area."

"No, there are not. . . ." I stopped in mid-sentence, remembering the phrase that Clarence had added . . ."with a big old bunched up collar." I said, "It just dawned on me. I think I know what he was talking about. What does a sailor wear that has a big old bunched up collar?" I answered my own question. "A pea coat. Clarence saw someone leaving who was wearing a Navy pea coat. To Clarence that meant a sailor."

Fleshman looked unconvinced. "But why wouldn't he just say he saw a man in a pea coat?"

"I don't know. Clarence's mind didn't compute like everybody else's."

Fleshman gave me a quizzical look. "So I should start looking for someone who has a pea coat? As a prime suspect in the Dean's murder?"

"Look. I'm saying that Clarence saw someone Sunday night and it looked to him like a sailor." I took a deep breath. "And I think that sometime later he saw that person again, *wearing a pea coat,* and made the connection."

He added, "Then Clarence might have told us who that was if he hadn't been killed."

We sat looking at each other for another long moment. Fleshman said, "Damn. Damn."

I said, "I should have asked him."

"Don't beat yourself up about it. You did what you could at the time. I'll call for backup and for crime scene techs. They will be here soon. I think it would be good if you just go home. If you want me to drive you, I can."

I dragged myself out of my chair. "You need to be here. I can make it by myself. But thanks."

He nodded, and with my legs feeling like wooden stumps, I slowly plodded out of the building, and managed to get in my car. I sat there for what seemed like a long time, but it was probably only five minutes before I could get my hands to do what was necessary to start the car. When I finally got my mind working, I guided the car at an ant's pace down the streets toward home. When I turned the corner, I saw Aunt Grace's convertible pulled up on the grass at the front of my house.

I drove past her car and steered the Honda carefully into my driveway. My arms were rigid, and I had to consciously program my feet and hands to do the simple task of stopping and parking the car.

Some kind of delayed reaction was setting in. I sat there, too tired to move, looking at the steely gray sky and the blackjack trees that lined the driveway, pointing their bony fingers upward. The cold wind whipped up the blackened leaves and tossed them on the dead grass, making a thick dark carpet. A line of poetry ran through my mind: "If winter comes, can spring be far behind?" This year, spring would be far, far behind. If it ever came again.

I thought about Clarence, and of how little I knew about him. He lived alone, somewhere in the northeast part of Oklahoma City. That was about all I knew for sure. I had no idea if he had any relatives who would claim his body and bury him. How would we find out?

What kind of a friend had I been to Clarence? I slid out of the car, walked tiredly through the garage and opened the kitchen door. Tess, a furry black and white and tan ball, shot between my legs. I glanced quickly to see where she was going.. She was crouched in a corner of the garage.

She and Aunt Grace have had a set-to.

I called out, "Aunt Grace, I'm here."

She stormed into the kitchen, her face pink, and her eyes snapping. "Where did that infernal cat go? I tell you, Constance, she's possessed. She launched herself at me from atop the stove, for no good reason, like a wild tiger. I barely managed to avoid being killed."

In spite of myself, I felt tears burning behind my eyelids. I said, "Why are you here?"

Concern wiped out her anger at Tess. She said, "That nice detective called me." She paused, watching me carefully. "He told me about Clarence."

"How in the world did he know . . . ?"

"To call me?" Her glance was cautious. She said, "After the Dean's death, I phoned him to check his credentials. We talked about the case and about you."

"Aunt Grace, how could you?"

"He was very polite. He appreciated that I was concerned about you."

"But Aunt Grace. . . ." I paused. It was useless to scold her.

She said, "You sit down. I'll fix you soup and a grilled cheese and you tell me about what happened to that poor retarded man."

"His name is, was, Clarence," I said. It seemed important that he be called by his name.

"And somebody killed him. He was there that Sunday night, wasn't he?"

"Yes."

"Then he *knew* something, and he was killed for it."

Things were so simple for Aunt Grace. You went from A to B and then to C if necessary, and you didn't fret. Never mind if your premise was correct or not.

"And you were there too," she added, a slight hesitation in her speech. Then she reached out and put her hand on my arm. I saw the fear in her eyes. "Constance, you must be careful . . ."

Her voice trailed off, but I knew what she was thinking. Suddenly all the energy drained out of me, and I slumped down at the kitchen table. The tears welled up and began to spill down my cheeks. I felt completely helpless to stop them. I was crying because of Clarence's death, but I was crying for reasons that went beyond what had happened today.

I couldn't untangle or explain those reasons, even to myself. But one thing I felt I knew for sure. Life did not need to be this hard.

Aunt Grace said, "Oh my dear," and put her arms around me. I wept silently for what seemed to be a very long time. When I finally stopped, Aunt Grace got a soft cloth, wet it, and gently wiped the tears away. She washed my flushed face.

Her eyes, usually sparkling with vigor, were quiet and concerned. "Will you be all right now?"

I nodded.

"What are you going to do?"

I said, "I don't know exactly. Help Fleshman if I can. I will not let this pass. Clarence didn't deserve to die."

"You are very angry, Constance."

"Yes," I said. I hadn't realized how angry I was. But it was a good feeling, burning away the shock, the fear, the sadness, and leaving me with a determination to do whatever I could to find Clarence's killer.

"You are also very stubborn. It wouldn't do any good to warn you to back off and leave these things with Detective Fleshman?"

"No."

"That's what I thought. "Then do be careful."

Chapter 10

I blocked off Sunday for myself. The phone rang twice, but I let the answering machine take the calls. One was from the <u>Daily Oklahoman</u> wanting details about Clarence's death, which I ignored. The other was from Aunt Grace telling me she was on her way to church and would see me later.

Late in the afternoon, Fleshman phoned. He said, "How are things going?"

"I'm better," I said. "I've spent most of the day sleeping. Don't know when I've been so tired."

"Shock and an adrenalin rush make you tired. You've had your share of both lately." He paused. "I wanted to let you know what's been happening. We've located the next of kin for Clarence, an uncle named Henry Daffron who lives in a small town east of Nashville. He'll pay to have the body sent there when we can release it."

So Clarence's last name was Daffron. Clarence Daffron. I hadn't known that, I had never bothered to ask.

He added, "The M.E. is working overtime to help us. We should have his final report soon. I wanted to ask a favor. Would you feel like meeting me tomorrow morning at the University?"

I thought about yesterday's aborted meeting. About the shock of finding Clarence. I realized he was being kind, wanting to be sure I could handle going back so quickly to the scene of Clarence's death. I said, "I can be there."

I wanted to help, and maybe going over the whole thing one more time would dredge up some detail that might have slipped my mind. It was worth trying.

Then I added, "Before you hang up, I need to fill you in

on a couple of things that have happened. They may be important.

"I got an unsigned e-mail a few days ago saying that the Dean got what he deserved and that I should keep my mouth shut, or else. Of course, I have no idea who sent it." I paused, thinking he might ask a question, but he was quiet.

I went on, "Then, something else happened, entirely unrelated to that. Vice President Munsell asked me at the funeral if Dean Stafford had given me any *special* file to keep for him. The Dean hadn't, and I explained that to Munsell, but I don't think he believed me."

That information seemed to pique Fleshman's interest. He asked "What exactly is Munsell's job as Vice President?"

I replied, "Actually, he has two jobs. He is Vice President of Financial Affairs and Academic Affairs. But he spends most of his time with finances, raising money for the University and the Foundation which he administers. Then he puts on his other hat, takes charge of academic affairs when someone is hired, or fired, or promoted."

"Hum," he said, "that's interesting. The money angle, I mean. Probably worth checking into."

"The money?" I was shocked. "Why? All the monies coming into and going out of the University are carefully monitored."

"What about the Foundation?"

"It gets a lot of extra money, and Munsell handles the day to day activities, but he's responsible to a Board of Directors."

"A money trail is always interesting to follow. I never discount the power of money to corrupt."

I laughed. You're a suspicious man, Detective Fleshman."

He interrupted, "Why don't you call me Jake?"

I finished my sentence. "But being suspicious probably makes you a good detective." I paused a half-second, and added, "And I'm glad you are a good detective, Jake."

He laughed and said "I'll see you tomorrow."

Chapter **11**

On Monday morning I was at the University at seven-thirty, but I checked the parking lot to be sure I wasn't alone before I got out and went inside. I saw several lights on in offices and I assumed other chairpersons were getting ready for the new semester.

I hurried into my room. I had some serious work of my own to do. One of the major tasks was checking enrollment figures to be sure that classes were balanced. That meant going over each instructor's schedule carefully.

Working steadily, I moved ten students into two of the smaller classes to be sure the quota of fifteen students was met, hoping the students wouldn't get too upset about having a different professor than the one they had chosen.

Changing schedules is a tricky business, and I was absorbed in the process when someone knocked at the door. I jumped, scattering the schedules all over my desk. I was expecting Fleshman, but I was still jittery from all that had happened and was still happening.

I wondered if I would ever again be able to walk the halls and sit at my desk without being frightened of my own shadow. Before I could get up for the door, Fleshman stuck his head inside and said, "You look very busy, Dr. Crashaw."

I sighed and said, "I am. But come on in. I came early to head off some problems. When classes begin it will be pandemonium around here."

He moved quickly into the room. As usual, he was impeccably dressed. This time it was a navy blue suit with red tie.

I motioned for him to sit down. Then I said, "Not only

are things generally chaotic with the beginning of a new semester, but it will be much more difficult now that we don't have a Dean."

He said, "I'm sure that's true, but won't the Powers That Be see to that problem?" He paused and asked "How does the vacancy get filled anyway?

"Vice President Munsell will appoint someone" I said. His Appointee will be a temporary Dean until all the paperwork of scouring the countryside for a permanent one is done."

"Any chance you'll be the one to fill in?"

"I will apply for it, and I've got all the qualifications the position calls for. But I don't know if that's enough to get me the job."

He smiled and said, "I hope it does. I think you would make a very fine dean

I forced a smile back at him said, "We will see."

I guess something in my face clued him in that I didn't want to talk any longer about that subject.

He said, "Would you like for me to get us coffee or something, before we start?"

I wanted to get the questioning over. I shook my head and said, "I'm ready for your questions right now. Maybe we can do coffee later."

He sat up and leaned forward, his eyes intent. "Okay, let's go over the whole thing from the time you got here until you found the Dean.

First, did you see anyone outside the building, in the parking lot, or walking around the building before you came inside?"

"No, but I wasn't paying much attention to anything but getting out of the weather."

"The doors are locked at night?"

"Always. Except when night classes are in session."

"But you have a key?"

"Yes, and so does everyone else who works here. The professors, maintenance people, secretaries."

"When you were in the building and walking to your office, you heard the Dean talking to someone? And a short time later you heard the argument begin?"

"Yes. I'd been in my office five or ten minutes. Long

enough to get out of my coat and turn on the computer."

"But you couldn't tell if it was a man or a woman arguing with him?"

"I couldn't."

"After the argument stopped, what happened?"

"I heard footsteps going past my office. I remember thinking that the Dean had been ripping someone apart. And I wondered if it were a professor or a student."

"Let's talk about the time frame when all this was happening. What time did you get here?"

"At 9:00 p.m. I remember looking at my watch and thinking that I had twelve hours exactly to get the schedules on the Dean's desk. The argument began around 9:15, and I got up and shut my office door. But I heard the footsteps when someone went past my door. I think It was about 9:25 by then.

"The person was going past your office and out the south door?"

"Yes."

"Then what?"

"I decided to go for coffee."

"And that's when you saw Clarence?"

"Yes."

"Where was he?"

"He was standing in the upper foyer, mop in hand, looking down at me."

"Do you have any idea how long he had been standing there?"

"No."

"Then it's possible that he had been there when the killer went out the south door?

"It's possible."

He said, "And if you hadn't shut your door, you might have seen who was leaving?"

"If I had glanced up, I probably would have."

"Back to Clarence. What did he say to you?"

"I mentioned the weather again, and he said he was still concerned about the 'winds a'joinin.'"

"Why do you suppose he didn't say anything about seeing a sailor?"

"That's easy. We were talking about the weather. You

have to remember that Clarence's mind was simple and his thinking was one-track. We were talking about the weather and that's what he was concentrating on."

"Okay. Then you told him you had to get busy and go back to work. Then you got your coffee and headed toward your office?"

"Yes."

"But you stopped, decided to go back and get coffee for the Dean and take it to his office?"

"That's right. I decided I'd make a good will gesture. Try to ease the bad feeling between us before the new semester began. We'd had quite a clash, and I knew it was up to me to make the first move."

Fleshman got up and began to pace back and forth. His coat was open, and I could see the badge on his belt. I caught a glimpse of his gun, and I was reminded again of how little I knew about his world, how remote violence had been from my life until now.

He stopped pacing and sat down, his eyes thoughtful. "Where would he go, do you think, after he left?"

"Who?"

"The murderer. After he went out the south door?"

I said, "He probably kept going south. It would have been easy for him to leave the campus, cross the street and vanish into a movie house, a bar, or a restaurant."

We both sat silent for a moment. Then I asked, "What do you make of all this?"

He ran his hands through his hair, a nervous gesture, and said, "I think the Dean was killed in a fit of passion by someone who knew him. I also think that maybe the person didn't plan to kill him, but something they argued about pushed him over the edge, and he did kill him."

I said, "And Clarence probably saw the killer. And some time later, he finally remembered about the pea coat and put it all together."

Before he could reply, his cell phone beeped. He flipped it open and said, "This is Fleshman."

As he listened to the voice on the line, he glanced at me. I started to move away, thinking that the call might be confidential, but he held up his hand and motioned for me to stay. Finally he

70

said, "You're sure about that?" He listened another minute and then said, "Okay. Thanks."

He put the phone back in his pocket. He didn't say anything immediately.

Then he looked at me and said, his voice quiet and thoughtful, "That was the Medical Examiner. Clarence was killed by a blow to the head."

My stomach knotted, and I looked away.

"But that's not all. He wasn't killed at the University. He was killed somewhere else."

"What?"

"The killer moved the body."

Chapter 12

"What?" I said again. "Clarence was killed somewhere else? His body was moved?" I sounded like a demented parrot as I stammered on, "But that doesn't make any sense!"

"The M.E.'s sure about it. His tests verified it. It has to do with how the blood settles in the body."

"But why?" I said. "Why would the murderer take such a chance?

"I don't know. It *was* risky. It must have been something absolutely imperative that made him do it."

"How could you move a body and not be seen by someone?"

"He must have brought the body in through the side door at night. It's a short distance from the street to the doorway, and this area is not very well lighted, so it could be done."

"That's absolutely bizarre," I said. "It sounds like we're talking about the script of a Mafia movie, not something that would happen in Oklahoma City."

My mind raced. "Whoever did it would have to be very strong to carry dead weight like that."

I winced even as I said the word *dead*. I hated to think of Clarence's body being dragged around as if he were a dead animal being hauled off.

Fleshman shrugged his shoulders and said, "It wouldn't be easy. But when the adrenaline kicks in, a desperate person can do unusual things."

I said, "But that pretty well eliminates a woman as the killer, doesn't it? A woman couldn't lift the body, could she?"

"It is absolutely possible. I've seen nurses who didn't weigh much over a hundred pounds lift a brawny two hundred pound man."

"But when we found him, we thought he had been killed here. I mean, there wasn't any sign that he had been dragged or anything."

"But now we *know* he was brought here *after* he was dead. That's what I've got to deal with."

'The crime lab technicians are going over every square inch of his room and the area outside. If we're lucky, we may find something."

I had to ask, "Do we know what time he was killed?"

"The M.E. estimated the time of death at approximately 5:00 or 6:00 p.m. Friday."

"And I talked to him about 8:30 that morning."

I was beginning to feel as if I had been catapulted into a Kafkaesque world where nothing made any sense.

"That means that after I talked to him, in span of eight or nine hours at the most, Clarence met someone who killed him. And then moved his body to make it appear that he was killed here. "

"It looks like that's it."

"That's insane."

"Not necessarily. In fact, it is a pretty good way for the killer to get rid of the body by putting it on campus where another murder had already occurred."

He added, "You also have to understand that murder is never a logical, *sane* act. It's usually done under deep emotional stress, and the result is usually messy and unpredictable."

"But how does that play out with Clarence the victim?"

He didn't answer for a moment. Then he said, "I think that the murder of Stafford was a passionate, violent act, and I think that Clarence was killed because he *saw* the murderer leaving the building."

I stared at him, long and hard. Then I said, "Then it was someone Clarence knew. It was one of us!"

The look on his face said it all. He agreed with me.

"This whole thing is making me sick," I said. And it was. My stomach was knotting up in a way that was becoming all too familiar.

"We'll find who did it, Connie. I hope sooner than later, but in the meantime I want you to be careful."

I said, "But I didn't *see* anything."

"I know that, and you know that."

I said, "But you're implying that the murderer may *not* be sure that I didn't see him."

If only I had not shut the door, or if I had been curious enough to open it when I heard the footsteps.

"My God, Jake, if he thinks I <u>did</u> see him . . . "

His eyes said it all. I let out my breath, hoping to loosen the muscles in my knotted stomach. It didn't help, but I managed a weak smile and said, "Then I *will* need to be careful."

Chapter **13**

After Fleshman left, I worked rapidly and finished the rest of the schedule changes in fifteen minutes. I grabbed my briefcase and stuffed my Shakespeare text and class notes in it. I wanted to get out of the building as fast as I could. I jerked on my jacket, snapped off the lights and opened the door.

Standing there, hand raised to knock, was Chris Herndon. My heart was trip-hammering and I blurted out, "My God, Herndon, you scared me."

"I'm sorry," he said, looking a bit taken aback. "I saw you come in a while ago, and I thought it might be a good time to talk. While the students are not here, I mean."

I was surprised that he wanted to talk. Usually he avoided me as if I were a leper so that I wouldn't be able to determine how drunk he was on any given day. Motioning him inside, I dropped my briefcase beside my desk and sat down. I didn't take off my jacket, hoping he would take the hint and make his stay brief.

He sat down and pulled out his cigarettes. "Mind if I smoke?"

I pushed an ash tray toward him and he lit up. His eyes darted around the room. I knew he wasn't sober. He was never completely sober. But it was hard to tell how drunk he was. He carried his liquor with aplomb, like the professional drunk he was.

He let out a thin stream of smoke and said, "Heard about Clarence." He paused a minute, focusing his eyes somewhere over my shoulder, and added, "Doesn't matter so much about the Dean, but it's a damned shame about Clarence."

"Murder is bad, no matter who is the victim," I said.

He stroked his thin face with one hand and flicked the ash from his cigarette with the other. He quickly added, "Oh, you're right about that. What I meant was, the Dean didn't have many friends, now did he?"

I didn't say anything, but I guess my look made him uncomfortable. He said, "Anyway, I'm glad I have a good alibi for Sunday night. Ed Parsons and I were tying one on at the Blue Boar that night. A lot of folks saw us there."

"Then you've got nothing to worry about, have you?"

"That damn detective keeps nosing around . . . "

I pushed my chair back. I had no intention of getting into a discussion with him about Fleshman, and my head was beginning to ache from the cigarette smoke. "If that's all, Dr. Herndon?"

His eyes narrowed, fox-like. "No that's not all," he said. "The rumor is that you're in the running for the job as the new Dean." He paused. "And if that's true, it might help if Ed and I were to let Munsell know we think you would be the best choice. Support from your colleagues would make a difference, if you know what I mean."

I knew what he was leading up to, but I wanted him to spell it out. "I see," I said, "and how would my being Dean help you?"

He took another deep drag on his cigarette. "Well, that's not the point. The point is that if you were Dean, I'd like to think you would support your professors when the chips are down."

"I always do . . . when they are in the right," I said. I stood up, and said again, "If that's all?" I hadn't said what he wanted to hear, and his sallow face showed his annoyance.

He ground out his cigarette and swayed to his feet. He moved slowly toward the door, hesitated a second and said, "Looks like Stafford made some serious mistakes. Got himself killed. He wasn't very smart, was he, Dr. Crashaw?"

He shut the door carefully. I stared at it. I had never considered Chris Herndon to be anything more dangerous than a drunk, intent on destroying himself. But he had just made me a not too subtle threat. That worried me. Was he just an annoying drunk, or was he capable of murder?

I tried to put his conversation out of my mind as I headed my car down the road to my house, but I couldn't, and as soon as

I got home, I phoned Matt. I hadn't seen him for several days, and I wanted to talk to him about Herndon. When he didn't answer, I left a message for him to call.

It was only six o'clock, but the sun was sliding down behind a bank of clouds, painting them a brilliant orange. I stepped out on the patio, a cup of coffee in my hand to watch the color fade and the dusk intensify into darkness.

The air was cold, but not bitter or cutting. I drank the coffee and thought about how drastically my life had changed. I had suddenly been removed from the isolated and intellectualized world of academia and thrust into a nightmarish world where suspicion reigned and nothing was what it seemed to be.

The protective shell I had crawled into after Eric deserted me had been cracked open by circumstances over which I had no control, and I felt naked and vulnerable. I shivered, took a final sip of coffee, and hurried back inside.

The phone was ringing. I was going to let the answering machine take the call, but then Matt said, "Pick up the phone, Con, it's me."

I grabbed it and said, "Where have you been?"

"Out of town. I kidnapped a cuddly eighteen year old from my class in Metaphysics on Friday. Drove to Dallas and spent the weekend doing you-know-what. Why do you ask?"

"Matt! Be serious."

"So you don't think I *could* make it with a young chick?" His laughter was contagious. I had to smile.

Then he said, "Okay I'm listening. What's been happening?"

"You've heard about Clarence?"

Immediately his voice sobered. "Yes, and it's a damn shame."

"But you haven't heard the latest. Fleshman just told me that whoever killed Clarence moved his body."

"What?"

I explained what the Medical Examiner had said. Matt's response was the same as mine had been. "That doesn't make any sense."

"I know. None of it makes any sense. Not the death of the Dean, and certainly not the death of Clarence."

"I agree," he said. "And what you need to do is back off

77

and let Fleshman do his thing."

"I know," I said. "But the waiting is making me jittery. Anyhow, do you want to come over for a drink? I've got an expensive bottle of bourbon a rich friend gave me."

He laughed. "Tempting, but I'm bushed. Give me a rain check?"

"Okay," I said, trying to keep my disappointment from my voice.

"See you later." He hung up.

I went into the den and turned on the artificial fireplace. I pulled out the bourbon from the cabinet, poured a couple of fingers over ice and took a deep swallow.

It was smooth and mellow, liquid gold. "Ahhh," I said, sighing. "Here's to the rich who make life so pleasant for their friends."

The phone jangled, and I grabbed it, thinking Matt had changed his mind.

It was Fleshman.

"I'll be out of town for a few days," he said. "I've got to go to Little Rock and testify in a murder trial." He paused. "And I wanted to tell you about two files our search at the Dean's house turned up."

Instantly my ears perked up. Maybe he had found the file that so concerned Munsell, the one that Munsell thought the Dean had given me

"They have to do with your two of your professors. One contains an official letter to Chris Herndon, signed by both the Dean and Munsell with copies to the Board of Regents. It's a formal notice that if Herndon is drunk again, either on the campus or in class, he will be immediately terminated."

So that's why Herndon was in my office today.

"The other file is on Eddie Parsons. He is being sued for sexual harassment by a student named Diane Connors."

I knew Diane. She was a beautiful and intelligent graduate student. Parsons was in deep trouble. She would be a formidable adversary.

He added, "The file contained a letter from Dean Stafford to Connors' attorney, saying he would testify in her behalf. Parsons got a copy of everything, of course."

"So these files makes both Herndon and Parsons

suspects?"

"It gives them a strong motive. I'll check their Blue Boar alibi again as soon as I get back."

He started to hang up.

I said, "Wait. Did you by any chance run across a file with my name on it? At the Dean's house, I mean?"

"No."

"Remember how Munsell keeps harping at me? About a special file he said the Dean had given me?"

"Sorry. Didn't find anything with your name on it." He paused. "I'll call when I'm back. In the meantime, you stay safe."

"Sure," I said. "You can count on it."

Chapter 14

The next day I had to decide if I were going to slink off and stay holed up, fairly safe from danger and trouble, or take a chance and see if I could do something to help Fleshman.

Aunt Grace had said I was both courageous and stubborn. It was the stubbornness that tilted me toward doing something. I didn't like being intimidated by my own fears or fears that others tried to lay on me. And I needed to make my move now.

When classes began on Monday, I would be swamped with the madness and chaos of a new semester, and it would be days before I could lift my head up to even look around.

That's why I found myself on campus at 6:00 a.m. the next day. Early morning was the best time to snoop around the LA building. Only one or two maintenance people would be there, and it was very unlikely that any professor would show up before 9:30.

I personally think it's a constitutional thing that keeps professors from ever being on campus early. Their brains, overstuffed with knowledge and oftentimes overheated with booze just don't kick into gear until the sun is high in the sky.

I unlocked the outside door and hurried inside. Only a few of the lights were on in the building, making the hallway shadowy. My heels rang loudly in the empty hallway as I strode toward my office.

It was eerily quiet and my heart began to beat a little faster. I remembered Jake's final words were "Stay safe." I was not exactly doing that by being this early at the place where two people had been murdered.

I slowed my pace and took several deep breaths, waiting for my courage to catch up with my stubbornness. It did, finally, but I was still glad when I reached my office.

I opened the door, and immediately I knew that someone had rummaged through my desk. I kept files on my desk in an order that I understood, and they had been moved around and then carefully placed back.

My first thought was that a student had been looking for old exams. I sat down and checked the desk where I kept class notes and examination papers filed. Nothing was gone.

I thought about Munsell, and his anxiety over the file from Stafford that he kept asking me about. *It could have been him, he has a master key.* That triggered another thought. *Maybe the file Munsell is looking for is in the Dean's office.*

I glanced at my watch. It was only 6:15. I had plenty of time to check the Dean's office before Nora got here. I had a key to her outer office where the duplicating machines were located.

If I were lucky, the door to the Dean's inner office could be unlocked. It was worth a try.

I looked up and down the hallway before I tried my key in the door. It opened and I scurried inside. I waited a minute for my eyes to adjust to the darkened room. I wasn't about to turn on any lights.

Quickly I went to the Dean's office and tested the door knob. It turned under my hand. I shut the door carefully behind me. Then I quickly crossed to the Dean's desk, sat down in his leather chair, and opened the file drawer.

The files were orderly and neatly labeled. Nora had seen to that, and I selected three of them, thinking I would examine them more carefully. But my hands were shaking, and I dropped them to the floor. I bent to pick them up and froze in place. I heard someone walking by the door.

I waited, sure that whoever was outside would burst in at any moment and catch me red-handed. A minute dragged by, and then another. I listened intently. Then I heard a door close down the hall.

I took two deep breaths, and unloosed my clinched hands. Then I carefully picked up the scattered files and waited a second longer. I examined them briefly. They contained letters, reports, memoranda, but nothing seemed important enough to warrant Munsell's concern. I put them back in the file cabinet.

I looked through the remaining files, searching for one with my name on it. Again, nothing. I turned to the credenza behind his desk and opened it, but it was empty.

I leaned back in the Dean's chair, trying to imagine where he might hide a file, if he had one he didn't want anyone to know about. The bookshelves were filled with leather-bound books that had been lined up in orderly precision. I stared at them, and then I thought. *Of course! If someone wanted to hide a file, what better place than behind a row of books?*

At the closest bookcase, I began groping behind the shelves. In my haste, I knocked three books off on the floor. When I knelt to pick them up, I heard the door to Nora's office open. I stood up quickly, book in hand, paralyzed in one spot.

It was Nora and she was saying, a puzzled expression on her face, "Dr. Crashaw, can I help you?"

I felt the blood rush to my face, and I thought to myself. *Damn. Damn. What had brought her in so early?*

I tried for casual. I said, "Oh, hello, Nora," and put two of the books on the desk. "You weren't here but the door was unlocked, and I needed a book the Dean had borrowed some time ago. I didn't think you'd mind if I picked it up."

I waved the book in my hand and added, "This is it, a reference book for my class in Shakespeare.

Her voice was polite. "Do you need anything else?"

"That's all for now," I said, moving toward the door.

I stopped in the doorway and looked at her. "I appreciate your work, Nora. If I should be appointed as the new Dean, I'm sure we will be able to work well together."

There was a slight change in her expression. She was smart enough to know that it would not be wise to ask any more uncomfortable questions if there were any chance I might be her future boss. "Of course," was her reply.

Back in my office, I re-grouped. My attempt at sleuthing hadn't worked out very well, but I had been able to get out of a sticky situation with minimum damage.

I wondered briefly if Fleshman ever flubbed up. I doubted that he did. He seemed so damnably efficient in every move he made.

I settled down at my computer with the book on Shakespeare by my side. I thought ruefully that I might not be a good detective, but I was a professional teacher and a very good one at that.

I was determined that this semester would be a challenging one for me and my students. I worked diligently for several hours, and finally shut the book, and leaned back in my chair.

The phone rang. It was Munsell's secretary. She told me that Dr. Munsell wanted to see me in his office as soon as possible. I sat staring at my desk while my mind kicked into high gear. *It's about the deanship; he's made his choice.*

In spite of a faint voice in my head warning me not to assume that I had been chosen, *another louder voice was saying, If he hasn't chosen me, why would he be calling?*

I got up, glanced in the mirror and decided the sweater and skirt I had on looked professional enough. The suede jacket wasn't particularly sharp, but I could take it off before I went into Munsell's office.

I walked across campus, taking in deep gulps of the fresh, clean air. The sun had struggled through the gray clouds and was warm on my face. The campus was deserted except for a few straggling students, one of whom waved at me.

I waved back. I was feeling good. Maybe my luck was going to change. Maybe the years of working for deans who were incompetent political appointees were going to end. Maybe I would be the first female dean on Harding campus.

It was an exhilarating prospect.

Munsell's secretary, an attractive blonde, smiled and told me to go right in.

I paused and smoothed my hair before I knocked on the door. Munsell opened the door, a smile on his face, and said, "Ah, Dr. Crashaw, thank you for coming on such short notice. I'm pleased I could catch you before you left today."

His smile seemed friendly enough, but his eyes were cautious and wary. I sensed tension in the way he squared his shoulders and rubbed his hands together before he motioned for me to sit down. "Would you like coffee or a coke?"

"No, thanks," I said. I would have liked coffee, but Munsell's tension was contagious, and I was afraid if I had a cup to handle I might spill it. I sat back in the leather chair and willed myself to relax.

"Are things going well in the English department?"

"I think so. Classes are full for the spring semester."

"That's a difficult department to chair."

I didn't know what to say to that. I wasn't sure if it was an indirect compliment or a subtle indictment. So I just nodded.

"The death of Dean Stafford has created some real problems. I think you realize that."

He got up and walked to the window. I wondered what particular problems he had in mind.

He said, more to the window than to me, "I've got to appoint a new dean before the semester begins."

Abruptly he moved from the window and sat back down behind his massive desk. His eyes, pale and searching, fixed on me. "I have to know that the new dean will work with me as closely as Dean Stafford did."

I kept my eyes level with his. I said, "I can understand that."

"The new dean and I will work together on some, ah, difficult problems, and it will be necessary that we be in agreement on how we handle them."

He raised his eyebrows and pursed his lips. His voice had taken on a pontifical whine as he added, "We *must* trust each other."

"Of course," I said. I was beginning to be very uncomfortable. *What in hell was he getting at?*

"And if either of us gets information, good or bad, that involves our partnership, we will, of course, share it, in confidence, with each other?"

The light came on. He was referring to the damned file I was supposed to have from the Dean, the one he thought I was refusing to give him.

I decided that I would tell him the truth one more time, make it clear that I had never received a secret file from the Dean. So I addressed his unspoken question.

I said, as forcefully as I could, "Dean Stafford did *not* leave any special file with me. More than that, I searched his office today to see if I could find one there. I didn't. His house has been inspected carefully by a team of experts. Other papers were found, but no file addressed to me. I *do not* have the file you are searching for." I sounded stilted and formal, but I hoped I had made my point clear.

His face was difficult to read. There was no flicker of

surprise that I had brought up the subject, and no discernible reaction to what I had said. His voice, when he spoke, was completely noncommittal. "I see."

He moved papers around on his desk and picked up a pencil. He tapped it on the arm of his chair for a second or two, and then looked at me. He said, "I need to ask you a few questions about how you see a dean functioning as a key administrator."

I nodded and said, "I'll be glad to talk to you about that."

He peppered me with questions for the next fifteen minutes. I answered them the best I could, but I knew the litmus test had been my statement about the file.

I hadn't the slightest clue if I had passed or not.

Finally he stood up and said, "Thank you for your time. I will be in touch soon."

Chapter 15

I walked slowly back across the campus. The excitement of going to Munsell's office had been replaced with a kind of brooding uncertainty about the outcome of my interview.

I vacillated between the hope that I would be named the new Dean and the fear that I had never been seriously considered for the job. I tried telling myself that whether or not I got the appointment, my life would go on. But that was cold comfort. I wanted very much to be Dean Crashaw.

When I got back to my office, there was voice mail from Aunt Grace. "Don't forget our dinner date. At the Victorian House. 6:30 sharp. Don't be late."

For once I was glad that I had a tea date with Aunt Grace. A frivolous talk with her would be a relief from all the tension I had been through today. I looked at my watch. It was 6:15 now and I would have to hurry. The Victorian House was one of the few downtown tea shops, and I'd have to drive like mad to get there on time.

The main streets were wet and slushy with a few patches of ice that made driving a bit tricky, but I made good time. My mind wandered back to the meeting with Munsell. The more I thought about it, the more convinced I was that I had been foolish to bring up the mysterious and elusive file.

I should have let it alone, or at least have waited until he point-blank asked me about it. Would I ever learn to be more political and, for God's sake, more *diplomatic?*

I pulled up in a parking space at the tea room and sat for a moment, trying to push aside the depressing thought that I might have blundered with Munsell. I looked at my watch. I was fifteen minutes late! Aunt Grace would be livid. I hauled myself quickly out of my car and headed for the door.

The tea room was crowded with little old ladies like Aunt Grace. I stood at the front, scanning the room, hoping she wouldn't have a serious agenda for my improvement on her schedule. I wanted to drink tea, stuff myself on dainty sandwiches and gooey sweets, and forget the worries of the academic world.

One of the owners, a tall black man, his wide smile disclosing perfect white teeth, came up and said, "Good afternoon, Dr. Crashaw, your Aunt is here." I remembered that Aunt Grace had introduced him, but I couldn't come up with his name. I smiled politely and followed along.

Aunt Grace was smiling, which was a good sign. She was not wearing her solemn-eyed-pursed-lips face that signified a lecture in the offing. "You're *almost* on time, Constance."

"The roads were slushy, and there were slick spots. I was careful."

"As you should have been." She raised her tea cup and said, "This is a new herbal tea recommended by Paul. Guaranteed to relieve tension and stress, and create a rosy aura around your distressed psyche."

She saw the look on my face and laughed. "In other words, it's good for what ails you." She was in an expansive mode.

I relaxed, smiled, and said, "Then I'll have a large pot of the stuff. I need it."

She didn't say anything while the waitress, a fluffy teenager with a cutesy apron, brought a fresh pot of tea. I watched the girl as she poured. She was careful, but she giggled when she finished. I wondered if I had ever been that young and giddy, and decided that I hadn't.

Aunt Grace, finger appropriately crooked, took a sip from her cup, sighed contentedly and, as was her usual custom, got right to what was uppermost on her mind. "Has the murderer of the Dean and that poor janitor been found?"

I took a sip of tea and said, "Maintenance man, Aunt Grace, Clarence was our maintenance man. He was much more than just a janitor."

I was surprised at the tartness of my reply, but it seemed important to me that Clarence's job, and his memory, be given

87

some dignity. I gentled my voice and added, "No one has been arrested yet."

"Detective Fleshman will find him, Constance. And soon. You will see."

I was about to agree with her when the waitress came with the tray of sandwiches, cheeses, and sweets. I was hungry. I hadn't realized that sleuthing could drum up such an appetite.

I loaded my plate with three of the tiny sandwiches and the cheese balls. Aunt Grace settled for the sandwiches. Between bites she said, "He's a very nice man."

I supposed she was still talking about Fleshman but I was not sure. I mumbled around the food, "Who? Detective Fleshman?"

"Yes, of course." She looked at me as if I were a recalcitrant student who hadn't been paying attention.

She said, "He has a very good background. Before he came to Oklahoma City, he was a Detective on the Boston Police force. He has a law degree from Boston University."

She paused and popped another tiny sandwich into her mouth. "He came here five years ago. He left Boston because of some political shenanigans that he couldn't stomach. He is a man of integrity."

I stopped eating and looked at her with complete amazement. She was reeling off personal information about Fleshman as if she were his biographer.

I said, "How in the world do you know so much about Detective Fleshman? You didn't find all this out in one phone call?"

She ignored the question completely.

"He is not married now. His wife left him just before he moved here, but their marriage had been in trouble for some time. She wasn't going to move to Oklahoma where she thought the Indians still ran loose in the streets."

She paused for a breath and added, "They didn't have any children. He's a very eligible man, Constance."

"Good God, Aunt Grace, you *didn't* find out all this with one phone call!"

"Don't curse, Constance, it's not becoming."

Her slipperiness in dodging an issue was maddening. "Aunt Grace, you're avoiding the question. How do you know all this about Detective Fleshman?"

She took a sip of her tea. "Doesn't this new tea have a piquant flavor?"

"Aunt Grace!"

"I talked to him. I took him to lunch and I talked to him."

She looked at me, her eyes rounded with a feigned innocence. "There is no law that says a seventy year old lady cannot invite a handsome fifty-five year old police detective to lunch."

I probably looked like a gaffed fish. My mouth was hanging open.

"You'd probably be surprised at how easy I am to inspire others to confide in me when I try. It's an art I developed so I could stay alive in public school teaching.

She added, "Detective Fleshman *likes me.* He said I reminded him of a special aunt . . . or was it his grandmother? I forget. Anyway, it was a pleasant lunch and he promised to keep a close watch on you."

I barely managed to stifle a groan. *There is no telling what else she might have told him that she's not telling me.* I resisted the urge to shake her until her teeth rattled.

What could I say to Fleshman to convince him that her impertinent questioning was a part of her quixotic personality, not something I had put her up to?

"He's the kind of man you need to be interested in."

I felt my face flush. I carefully placed my tea cup down in front of me, and said, "Don't even *think* about it, Aunt Grace."

"About what?"

"You know what. About trying a little match-making."

I took a quick gulp of tea and gave her what I hoped was a baleful stare. I said, "Remember the last time?"

"Well, it could have worked out."

"It could have worked out only if I had been interested in an arrogant Methodist preacher who thought women should be subservient to patriarchal males and never, never, question any religious dogma. Honestly, Aunt Grace."

"All right, it didn't work out. But Detective Fleshman is different."

I stopped her. "Detective Fleshman is an excellent policeman and he and I are friends. But that's all. Now will you please stop trying to make something else out of it?"

She changed the subject, another clever way of getting me confused. She said, "You know you look very much like your mother when your color is up, Constance. She was a beautiful woman. You are too."

I sighed. I knew when I was licked. I took another sip of my tea to keep my mouth busy but quiet.

After we finished lunch, I paid the check and left Aunt Grace in deep conversation with Paul the owner. I managed to get her attention long enough to say goodbye. She responded with a wave of her hand.

I got into my car, wondering if I would ever be a match for Aunt Grace's maneuvering.

I left the parking lot and pulled into the line of traffic, which had lessened considerably. Most of the downtown workers had made their way out of the city and into the surrounding suburban areas that swallowed them up for the weekend.

I had planned to go directly home, but I realized I had left my briefcase in the office with the new Shakespeare book in it. I deliberated whether to go back to the campus for it, and finally decided that I needed it to at least to do a short study before Monday.

I hurried from my car into the building and almost ran down the hall to my office. I quickly unlocked the door, looked for my briefcase, got it, and turned around to flip off the lights.

I was out of the door and locking it when I saw a former student with a girl hanging on his arm, walking down the hall toward me   It was Aloysius Jones, captain of the soccer team. I didn't know the curvy co-ed.

Aloysius was a broad shouldered, amiable jock, who was barely able to maintain the grade point necessary to keep him eligible for sports. I had had dealings with him before. He always squeezed into Boyd Finnell's classes to get an easy A.

I supposed he was late in enrolling and needed permission to get in Finnell's literature class.

He said, "Can we see you a minute, Dr. Crashaw?"

I sighed, turned the lock in the door, and motioned them into the office. I put my briefcase on my desk and sat down. I looked out of the window at the sun streaking the sky with pink and gray and blue, wishing I could be on my way home before the cold and the dark took over. I skipped the amenities and got right to the point.

"What's your problem, Aloysius?" He was nervously shifting his weight from one foot to another while stealing anxious glances at his girlfriend. She was nodding her head and blinking her eyes in what I assumed was her way of telling him to get on with it.

"We need to, uh, tell you something."

I realized I wasn't going to get rid of them quickly. "Okay. What do you need to tell me?"

I had assumed he had scheduling problems, but it could be something else, a conflict with a professor, a problem about a grade, or a personal problem.

In spite of their sophistication, students come up with horrendous personal dilemmas. In the past I had heard confessions of every known sin along with justifications for every kind of devious conduct known to the human race.

These two looked guilty enough to need absolution. Aloysius collapsed into the nearest chair. His girlfriend perched next to him, looking as if she might take flight any moment.

He swallowed two or three times then blurted out, "It's about Dr. Finnell and Sunday night. When we was supposed to be with him."

He pulled himself upright and leaned forward, his hands locked tightly together. His voice was apologetic. "Well, we wasn't with him *all* the time, you know what I mean?"

I didn't know what he meant, so I asked, "What do you mean ''you weren't with him all the time?'"

He said, "Well, we left to get a hot dog a little before 9:00, maybe fifteen minutes or so before, and then we went to the car to get her coat, and then, well, we didn't go right back to the game." His voice trailed off.

I got the picture. They had been in the car, making out, and had forgot all about the basketball game. "How long before you got back?"

His face reddened and he stared at his Nikes "Oh, about forty or forty-five minutes later."

"It was an hour." This from the girl friend.

"Why are you telling me this?" I asked.

Aloysius said, "Because that detective's been back asking us questions. I don't think he believed what we been telling him, and we're afraid we're in trouble."

"You told Detective Fleshman you were with Dr .Finnell *the whole time that evening,* and now you're telling me that's not true?"

They both nodded.

Damn. If they're telling the truth, then Finnell is in trouble with his alibi. I said, "Have you told anyone else about this?"

Aloysius, still looking nervous, said, "We tried to call the Detective. Couldn't get him."

"Have you seen Dr. Finnell? Or talked to him about this?"

They shook their heads. "Then don't. You understand?" I saw the indecision on their faces. They were having second thoughts about having snitched on Finnell.

I added, "Detective Fleshman is out of town for a day or so, but when he gets back, Dr. Finnell can sit down with him and tell him exactly where he was during that time."

Aloysius' liquid brown eyes showed concern. "We don't want Dr. Finnell to get in no trouble."

I stood up and moved around the desk toward the door. "You did the right thing, Aloysius." I said, as I herded them out.

I wondered what Fleshman would do when he heard that Finnell's perfect alibi was now seriously impaired.

I was sure he would pull Finnell back in for some serious questioning. He might even arrest him. That thought brought a smile to my face.

I watched Aloysius and girl-friend friend scuttling down the hallway, deep in conversation, then I picked up my briefcase, closed the door to my office, and hurried down the hallway and out of the building.

It was completely dark, and the tall orange lights threw a garish light on the parking lot. I walked quickly to my car, jumped inside, and locked the doors.

Leaving the campus, I drove slowly past the Blue Boar. The parking lot was full. It was a favorite watering hole for students as well as the forty-something executives who worked in downtown Oklahoma City and lived in the wealthy homes west of the university.

I thought about stopping for a drink to ask some discreet questions about Chris Herndon and Eddie Parsons and what they had been doing there the night the Dean was murdered.

But I decided against it. My previous sleuthing had got me into trouble, and I didn't want to push my luck again. And it was beginning to look like Finnell was the number one suspect.

The traffic ahead of me suddenly slowed and came to a standstill. I could see whirling blue and red lights of police cars.

It was probably a wreck, and I became impatient. I took a right turn into an alley and sped over to a parallel street. Then I intersected the road I often took when I wanted to take a more peaceful, if longer, route home.

I could see the tail lights of a few cars, but they were far ahead. I turned on the tape deck, put in my newest Streisand, and relaxed.

I had driven about three miles when I became aware that a car behind me had its bright lights on. Irritated at the driver's lack of consideration, I clicked the rear view mirror to dim the reflection and slowed down, hoping he would pass.

Instead of passing, however, the car slowed, staying just behind me. I speeded up. It did too. My throat tightened. The road was not well-traveled, and the lights from Oklahoma City seemed very far away.

I tried to put the best read on the situation that I could. It could be a smart-ass kid wanting to show off, or an irate worker in a hurry to get home.

I jammed my foot down on the accelerator. The Honda responded and for a moment I thought I would be able to pull away from the other car. But I heard the roar of a powerful motor, and the car quickly closed the distance between us.

"He's going to hit me," I thought just before I felt his bumper slamming into the back of my car. The shock jerked my neck forward and then backward, and I gripped the wheel, fighting for control.

Another jolt spun me toward the shoulder of the road, and I felt the car begin to slide. It seemed as if I were in a slow-motion nightmare. I felt the car skidding sideways and plowing up snow in its slide toward the deep, snow-covered ravine on the side of the road.. Clinging tightly to the wheel, I braced myself, and at the last moment, I jerked the car back to the left. It responded by spinning around in a half circle and I ended up facing the opposite direction with the car wheels a hair's breadth from the edge of the ravine.

"*If I had plummeted into that ravine. . . .*" I couldn't stop shaking. The car that had jammed me sped by, motor roaring, a dark blur that vanished into the night.

When I finally had my wits about me enough to open my car door, I got out and leaned against it, legs trembling, gulping the cold night air to calm my nerves and clear my head. I glanced at the ravine that I had barely missed and shuddered.

I looked at the stars, bright against the blackness of the night, and let out a shaky sigh of relief. Rain had begun to fall and the lights of the city looked even farther away than ever. It was so quiet that I imagined I could hear the raindrops splashing into the banked snow alongside the road.

I stood there for a minute or two longer, letting the rain cool my face and letting my heart slow down to normal.

Then the fear that had been controlling me gave way to anger. "*Some damned teenager trying to show off,*" I thought. "*Or worse still, some damned adult, mad because I had passed him.*"

I wanted to hit somebody, but I saw the lights of another car approaching in the distance, so I got back in the car. I waited until he passed then pulled over to the right and headed down the quiet road.

When I got to the main highway, traffic was flowing smoothly. I pulled cautiously into the line of cars, for once glad for the traffic and the safety of numbers.

Chapter 16

When I got home, Tess was waiting at the door for me, meowing plaintively because I was late for her evening meal. She marched alongside me into the kitchen, tail high, intent on keeping me on track until her bowl was filled.

When I had her settled down, I headed for the bathroom, filled the tub with hot water and fragrant bubbles, and sank down in it with a sigh. I had soaked for at least fifteen minutes, feeling the tension gradually melting away when Tess, having finished her gourmet fish dinner, came into the bathroom. She leaped on the table beside the tub and gazed at me with a questioning look.

"You'd soak too, if you had just been run off the road and almost killed."

She stared back, her slit eyes unwavering.

"I was scared, Tess, but I'm not going to crawl into a hidey hole and disappear. I'm not going to change what I do and where I go just because some creep tries to run me off the highway."

She stared impassively a moment longer, then, as if she had heard all she could stand, dropped her head and curled up into a tight ball.

Thanks a lot," I said and slid deeper into the warm bath. I sat in the water, my mind in neutral, until my fingers began to shrivel.

I sighed and scrambled out of the tub, flicking water on Tess, who gave me a disdainful look and pranced out of the room. I wrapped up in my warm bathrobe and padded barefoot to the den. I turned on the fireplace, poured a potent bourbon and water, and sank into a chair.

The phone rang and I jumped, almost spilling my drink.

It was Fleshman. I said, "You're back in town?"

"Yes. The Judge postponed the trial, and I will need to go back next month." He paused. "Just thought I'd check to see how things are with you."

"Well," I said, "which story do you want to hear first, the scary one or the suspicious one?"

"What do you mean?"

The bourbon was warming my stomach, and loosening my tongue. I said, "I'll start with the scary one."

I launched into the car incident, trying to act cool about it. I don't think I succeeded too well. My voice kept sliding high and then down low.

When I finished, he said, "You have to be more careful."

"I *was* being careful." I responded tartly. He wasn't being very comforting.

He said, "Did you get a glimpse of the car that hit you? Do you have any idea who it was?"

My voice sharpened. I said, "I was too busy trying to stay out of a ravine to pay much attention to what kind of a car the idiot was driving."

Then I realized I was sounding like a shrew. "Sorry, I said, 'I didn't mean to be sarcastic, but the whole thing is maddening. About the car - - I think it was dark and big, certainly bigger than my Honda."

"Okay," he said.

I imagined he was writing down what I was saying, but I knew as well as he did that hundreds of cars were big and dark and on the road at night.

"You said there was a scary thing and a suspicious thing. What was the suspicious thing?"

"It looks like Finnell's alibi is full of holes." I told him about the visit from Aloysius and his girlfriend.

He listened until I finished and then said, "Have you seen Finnell? Talked to him?"

"No, but I'm sure I'll see him Monday."

"Don't say anything to him about this, okay?"

"If you say so."

He paused and added, "Have you thought of anything new? About the night the Dean was killed, I mean?"

"No. I've worked my poor brain overtime trying to come

up with something. But I've told you everything that I can remember."

"Then don't fret, don't push too hard. And I'll see you soon."

I dropped the phone in its cradle and sat down on the couch before the fireplace, twirling the ice in my drink. Talking to Fleshman was fairly reassuring, but when I finished my first drink, I poured another one, doubling the bourbon.

It didn't take long for the drink to do its work. My arms became heavy and languorous, and I stretched my legs out comfortably in front of me, welcoming the feeling of lassitude and apathy. I wanted the bourbon to smooth the sharp edges of the day, remove the fear and anxiety that still clung to me.

It helped, but it didn't blur everything. The sound of the heavy car hitting my bumper and the fear that had throttled me flashed into my mind. A hair's breadth, just a hair's breadth, and I would have ended up in that black ravine, either dead or seriously hurt. I took another long swig.

The phone rang. I waited for the fifth ring before I picked up the receiver, and I waited another second to respond. My tongue was getting thick and my hello was a little mushy.

It was Matt. He said, "Con, what the hell? Where have you been?"

"Oh, I was driving home, and I took the long way around because of a car wreck, and I got in a kind of a predicament. I emphasized *predicament* by making four syllables out of it.

"Are you drinking? You're sounding pretty mushy."

Apparently Matt was too dense and dull-witted to appreciate my attempt at being humorous. "I'm not drunk, thank you. But I am drinking. Had a couple of double bourbons and waters, that's all."

That didn't come out exactly right , so I decided to put the questioning back on him. I said, "Where've you been, Matt?"

"More to the point, where have you been? I called your office earlier, no one answered."

I detected the weariness in his voice, or it might have been irritation. It didn't matter. I still had the warm glow from the bourbon.

Being careful to enunciate my words carefully, I said, "Well, I was taking the long way home and someone decided to tag my bumper with his bumper, and I . . ." I paused and added, "Wait just a minute, I need to freshen my drink. Then I'll tell you all about it."

His response was short and sweet. "I'm coming over."

" I'll make you a drink," I said to the dead phone. I mixed another bourbon and water and sipped on it before I made a gin and tonic for Matt. I had just put his drink on the bar when the doorbell chimed.

I picked up my glass, took another deep pull, skirted around Tess who had flattened out in front of the fireplace, and walked a bit unsteadily toward the door. I had a little difficulty getting my eye focused on the peep hole, but I wasn't about to let anyone in without checking first.

"Just a minute," I said. I put the drink on the floor, placed both hands against the door, and looked again. This time I could see it was Matt. I opened the door with a flourish.

Matt loomed large in the doorway. His hair was mussed, and he had on his favorite brown leather jacket. I thought he looked especially handsome. He picked up my drink, took me gently by the arm and said, "You're way ahead of me. I'll hold on to this until I catch up."

I didn't care. The room was tilting slightly, and I wasn't too sure footed. It might be better if he kept the glass until I sat down. His arm around my waist felt good as he guided me into the den where he deposited me in the large arm chair next to the fireplace.

"Your drink is over there," I said, waving my hand in the general direction of the bar. "You might freshen mine a bit while you're at it."

I smiled as graciously as I knew how. It's always wise to be pleasant to the drink-bringer-over, especially when you don't have the ability to get up and get the drink yourself.

He got his drink, handed me my glass, which I could see had not been refilled, sat down on the couch and said, "Now tell me what happened. Where were you? Who played tag with your car?"

"Well," I said. "It's like this." I began a rather long and rambling account of what had happened. Matt was patient. When I finished, he said, "Did anyone follow you out of the parking lot?"

I shook my head. "I don't think so. Fact is, there weren't many cars there -- one or two maybe."

He asked, "Where did you go after you left the university?"

"Well, I drove slowly by the Blue Boar. But I didn't stop. Thought I'd do that scene later on." I held up my glass, gave him what I thought was a very appealing glance and said "I'd really like another drink."

In his best no-nonsense voice he said, "Not right now."

"Well, okay, but you know what, Matt?"

"What?"

"I think I must have seen something that night when the Dean was killed."

"Did you? See anyone, anything?"

"Or maybe I didn't *see* anything; maybe I *heard* something." The booze had not only loosened my tongue but it was apparently doing something to my thinking process as well.

Maybe my subconscious had appreciated the bourbon and had decided to dredge up some meaningful stuff. Or maybe I was drunker than I thought, and I was talking nonsense.

Matt's eyes were somber. He was taking me seriously. I decided I'd better get a grip. What the hell *was* I talking about? I said, "I don't know, Matt. I'm really confused. And I guess everything is just shifting around in my mind."

I sighed. I was really tired, and I could not talk anymore. My tongue had suddenly turned into a thick, ropy thing, much too big for my mouth.

"Okay, Con." He stood in front of me, reached for my hands and pulled me up. "That's enough for tonight. It's off to bed for you. I'll hang around until you go to sleep."

I didn't argue. Matt always knew the right thing to do.

Chapter 17

I awoke the next morning with a pounding headache and a furry tongue. I slid to the side of the bed and raised my body up very slowly and carefully.

I had the feeling that if I moved too quickly my head might go spinning off into space. I put my head between my hands, pressed it very hard, thinking that the pressure might force it back into it proper size. It felt like a hard, overgrown watermelon.

In addition to the hangover, I was sore with strained muscles from having wrestled so desperately with my car last evening. I shuddered, remembering again how frightened I had been when the strange car slammed into me.

I finally stood up, and the headache accelerated into such a vicious pounding that I thought my skull might crack wide open.

I stumbled into the bathroom, tossed back three aspirin, chased by a glass of cold water. I clung to the basin, waiting to see if my stomach was going to handle the water and aspirin. It did, thank God.

I looked in the mirror, didn't like what I saw, and turned aside. I tried, unsuccessfully, to remember what the whole evening had been about, but it was foggy. Too much bourbon tends to make one feel good at the time, but terribly sorry about it all later.

I faintly remembered that Matt had tucked me in bed and said he would hang around until I got to sleep. I think I must have passed out as soon as I got horizontal.

Now I was in dire need of coffee. I choked back the nausea, struggled into my bathrobe, and took a few unsteady steps into the hallway. I looked around for Tess, wondering why she hadn't waked me.

Generally when I overslept she would jump on the bed, begin a pitiful meowing which quickly accelerated into a scream if I didn't respond fast enough. I plodded toward the kitchen, hoping that a cup of strong coffee would humanize me. I passed the kitchen stove and out of the corner of my eye I saw a blur of movement. Before I could compute what was happening and dodge out of the way, a bundle of spitting fur landed on my shoulder.

"Damn," I said, as I felt Tess's claws sink into my shoulder. I remained absolutely still. I knew if I made any attempt to dislodge her, she would only dig her claws in deeper.

"Nice kitty, nice kitty," I said, in the most soothing tone I could manage. "Take it easy, Tess." Her response was a low guttural sound and a tightening of her claws.

She was furious. I kept my shoulders rigid and very, very slowly inched my way toward the kitchen table. I eased down into a chair, both to keep Tess calm and my head from splitting.

"All right, Tess. I'm late with your breakfast, and I'm sorry. But I can't get you any food unless you turn me loose." I waited, scarcely breathing.

Then suddenly she sprang from my shoulder to the kitchen table. She stood directly in front of me, fixing me with a malevolent stare out of her slitted black eyes. I thought, *Aunt Grace may be right; this cat looks demonic.* Taking a deep breath, I said, "It'll be ready in seconds."

She flicked her tail, a sign of impatience. I moved as quickly as I could, trying not to jar my pounding head, opened a can of sardines, and shoved them into her feeding tray. The sharp, oily smell caused my stomach to churn, and I turned my head quickly aside.

Tess had been watching, and she gave me another sidelong glance before she jumped from the table and began to eat. I reached down and whacked her as hard as I could on the rump. "That's for being mean and nasty, Tess. I don't need any garbage from you." She flicked her tail, but kept her face in the food.

After such a hellish beginning, I was sure my day couldn't get worse. I dreaded going to the office feeling as rocky as I did, but I didn't have any choice.

The enrollment figures for the spring semester would be on my desk, and I had to make a comparison of this enrollment with the past three semesters and the report had to be on Vice President Munsell's desk the next day.

It was a PR thing with him. He wanted to put out quickly the news of any increase that we might have. I had no intention of being late with his report.

My head was still throbbing and I was feeling a bit feverish by the time I got to the campus. I walked toward the building, determined to get the report done as quickly as possible and get back home. The wind was freezing cold, and I began to cough. My chest hurt, partly from sore muscles, but I wondered if I were catching a cold, which was something I didn't need. Not with a new semester about to begin.

I hurried inside the building. The rush of warm air caressed my frozen face and my cold hands, but I still felt chilled.

I hugged my coat closer as I walked down the hallway. Lew Hawkins was standing at the coffee machine, his back to me. He looked like a gangly high school kid. He was wearing a worn corduroy coat and ill-fitting gray slacks. His hair, thin on top, straggled down the back of his bony neck.

I said, "Hi, Lew, how's it going?" but I kept moving. I had no desire to talk to him.

His eyes narrowed when he saw me and he said, "Ready for the next semester?" What he really wanted to know was if I had heard anything from Munsell about who would be the new Dean, but I had no intention of stopping to chitchat with him about that.

"Ready as I can be," I said, turning the corner before he had a chance to say anything more.

When I got in my office, I went to the small refrigerator in my secretary's office and rummaged around until I found two wizened lemons. I squeezed the juice into a cup, heated water in the coffee maker, and mixed it with the juice, which I laced with salt.

I popped two more aspirin and sipped the lemon-water concoction slowly. It was an old remedy Aunt Grace had used on me countless times when I had a cold. I didn't know if it was the acid from the lemon or the hot salty water, or if I just expected that it would help, but for whatever reason, my throat felt less scratchy and my headache relented enough that I could think.

My most pressing concern was to prepare the report for Munsell. The figures danced before my eyes, but I kept at it, and gradually the report began to take shape.

Someone knocked on the door, and I glanced at my watch. I'd been working for two hours. I picked up the lemon drink and swallowed the last of it. It was tepid, and the salt stung my mouth.

I grimaced. The knock sounded again.

I thought it was probably Boyd Finnell who usually made a point of coming by my office at the beginning of every new semester, not only to brag about how his large class enrollment was but also to check on me.

My first impulse was to keep quiet and hope that he would go away. But the knocking continued, so I pushed back from my desk. It would be easier to listen to him pat himself on the back now than to give him another excuse to say that I was never in my office. I walked to the door and opened it.

It was Lew Hawkins. He stood there, looking more like a reincarnated Ichabod Crane than ever. His hair was standing wildly on end, and his eyes, behind the wire-framed glasses, were beaming.

I think I knew what he was going to say before he opened his mouth. His smile was broad, and he squared his bony shoulders. "Guess what? Vice President Munsell just phoned. He has appointed me the new Dean of Liberal Arts."

My face felt stiff and I found it difficult to move my lips, but I heard myself saying, "Then congratulations are in order." The words were purely a reflex action, welling up from somewhere deep inside, prompted by a fierce desire to keep my pride intact. I would not let him know how upsetting his news was.

He came in and sat down, still smiling. I had no idea why he wanted to talk to me unless it was to gloat over his promotion. I had no respect for him. I had never seen him take a stand on any significant problem.

He waited until he saw what the consensus of the group was and then, and only then, did he chime in and give assent to the popular choice.

Aunt Grace would classify him, in her antique jargon, as a time-server and a boot-licker.

He said, "I guess all the times I've supported the goals and ideas of VP Munsell have paid off." He smiled expansively. "He knows he can count on me to back him up."

"You're right about that, Dr. Hawkins," I heard myself saying caustically. You'll never give him any trouble about anything."

His face reddened slightly.

"That's true. I don't consider it my job to tell an administrator, who is also my boss, what to do."

I said, "Not even if you know his decision is wrong-headed?"

I was baiting him. I wanted him to get angry. I needed to vent some of the frustration I was feeling, and I thought a rip-roaring verbal fight might do the trick.

He stood up and nervously ran his hand through his sparse hair. His look was spiteful and he said, "I'm not as all-knowing, as all-seeing, or as *bravely* contentious as you are, Dr. Crashaw."

Moving to the door, he paused and said, "But I *am* the new Dean. I *will be* the one who will or will not recommend your request for promotion to full professor." He was out the door.

I got up and locked it behind him. I sat down at my desk, and the magnitude of what had happened swept over me.

Not only would I have another incompetent and self-serving Dean to deal with, but Hawkins would be a rubber stamp for whatever Munsell wanted.

That meant that I could kiss my request for promotion good-bye. As long as Munsell thought I was lying about Dean Stafford's mysterious file, I didn't have a chance. The whole situation made the bile rise up into my mouth, and I was gripped by a deep and consuming anger.

"It isn't fair, it isn't fair," I heard myself saying fiercely to an empty room. That was when something hardened deep within me and the idea of how I could do something to make things turn for my advantage and for my benefit, came clearly into my mind.

I thought about Munsell and his continued concern for finding the file that he was positive Stafford had given me. It was certainly clear that he *believed* such a file existed, and that it was imperative that he get it into his hands.

"So," I thought, "why not change my story and tell him that I do have such a file. I can make it very convincing if I say that Dean Stafford insisted that he was trusting me to keep the file safe and secure, and that meant no one else was to see it."

My mind was whirling along a mile a minute as the plan kept developing. I thought, 'What if I use the non-existent file as a bargaining chip? He gets the file when my promotion to full professor comes through?"

"It will work," I said to the empty room. "Munsell has the power to make it happen."

"I will do it. I will get what I deserve."

"Not ethical, not moral, Connie," another voice said.

I responded. "Neither is what has happened to me,"

Chapter 18

Driving toward home, I went over again my plan to tell Munsell I had the file he wanted. The more I thought about it the more convinced I was that it was the only way I would ever be promoted to full professor. I spoke angrily to myself, *"And I deserve that much at least!*

Then another persuasive voice replied, *"You're right. Connie. You do deserve it, but. . . . but think again about how you are planning to get that promotion. Is that really you?"*

I shut out both voices. I didn't want to hear any dissenting voice and I didn't want to argue with myself any more.

My mind was made up. I was going to do what I had planned to do.

By the time I finally arrived home, the shock of Hawkins' promotion was wearing off and my anger had turned into a kind of depression, coming from all the anxiety and confusion of the past few hours.

I wanted to confront Munsell and tell him what a scheming, unconscionable low-life he was. But I knew that would be a foolish thing to do. He would simply justify his choice by some mealy-mouthed and devious reasoning. And I would lose my temper and shout at him, giving him a legitimate reason for reprimanding me.

"Keep cool, Connie," I said to myself. "Outsmart the bastard."

I needed to talk to Matt. He would understand and be as angry as I was. I could hear him saying, "By God, I'll go over and beat the hell out of Munsell," which I would certainly not let him do. Nevertheless, I felt better, just thinking about how Matt would respond.

When I got home, Tess met me at the door, and for a change she was quiet and mellowed. She rubbed my legs and followed me uncomplaining into the den where she jumped on the ledge of the fireplace, sat down, and watched me.

I dropped my briefcase and coat on a chair and picked up the phone to call Matt. I wondered if he might have taken the weekend to fly to Holyoke to see Annette before the new semester began. I tried to think if he had mentioned it to me, but I couldn't remember.

Gradually my anger lessened, leaving me physically tired and drained from the emotional roller-coaster I had been on. I hadn't eaten anything since breakfast, but I wasn't hungry.

I thought about mixing a stiff drink but decided against it, at least for the moment. The last thing I needed was to get smashed. I had enough control to know that drinking myself into oblivion wouldn't solve anything.

But the depression was settling in, like a black, suffocating cloud, and I was feeling that I was a loser again. I had lost the Deanship to a man who was both incompetent and stupid.

Just as I had lost Eric to a young bimbo whose vapid smile and big boobs had been irresistible. Five long years had not completely wiped out the horrible feeling of abandonment Eric's leaving had caused.

In the same way, I knew that the passing of time would not erase my feelings of anger and frustration over losing my chance to become dean. I *knew* that Eric was a lightweight, not worthy of the agony he had caused me, and I *knew* that Munsell was a fool, who deserved both my contempt and loathing, but that knowledge brought no solace.

I had been rejected. Again.

I sat staring into the fireplace, wondering how long it might be before I reached for the bourbon bottle. The ringing of the phone was a welcome relief. I reached for it, sure it was Matt.

"Matt?" I said.

"No, this is Fleshman."

"Oh," I said, unable to keep the disappointment out of my voice. I had wanted it to be Matt more than I had realized.

He caught the feeling. "Is this a bad time for me to be calling?"

"No," I said, "It's just been a really bad day."

"I can call tomorrow."

"No, of course not."

"Okay. I have a question. "Who beside Clarence would have a key to get into the building at night?"

The question surprised me. I said, "Well, everyone who had a key to the outside door, which means everyone. "It is only the professors' offices that have special keys."

"Would anyone other than Clarence have a key to his room?"

"I don't think so, but I don't know for sure."

" We found his room key in his pants pocket."

I said, "Then I guess someone else did have a key to his room."

"Any ideas?"

I thought a minute. My mind drew a blank. "I have no idea."

"Well thanks anyway."

He paused. "Had a bad day at the office, did you?"

"One of the worst."

"Sorry." Another long pause. Then he said, "Would a change of scenery help? A short ride into the country?"

I was surprised. I liked Fleshman, but I had never driven anywhere with him except, of course, on that awful visit to tell Helen Stafford the Dean was dead.

I hesitated, but only for a brief moment. He was being kind, and anything would be better than sitting around chewing on my innards and getting more and more despondent.

I might even be able to talk to him about Munsell. I had a feeling that he had probably dealt with Munsell types in his time.

So I said, "Okay."

"I'll pick you up in thirty minutes. Wear warm clothing, a sock cap, and boots."

I was glad for the chance to get out of the house. I hurriedly slapped a bologna sandwich together and ate it while I opened a can of tuna for Tess. She eyed me and the tuna speculatively, wondering, I supposed, why the treat.

I told her. "You're being pampered, Tess, because we feminine types have to hang together. Your mistress just got slapped back into the proper subservient position by the good ole boys, and I need your moral support."

Her face was in the tuna, but I'll swear she looked up at me and grinned.

True to his word, Fleshman was at the door by the time I had changed into warm woolen trousers and a sweater. I was stuffing trouser legs into my cowboy boots when the doorbell sounded. I paused long enough to check the peep hole before I let him in. There was no point in taking any chances.

We got into his Jeep. I didn't ask where we were going. I really didn't care. We headed north on highway 76, a small two lane road leading out of the city.

A few patches of snow reflected in the headlights, but travel had cleared most of the snow away. The warmth of the car and the quietness of the night comforted me. I relaxed against the seat, grateful that I didn't feel compelled to talk unless I wanted to.

It was a nice night. The winter moon, a round, metallic circle in the black sky, flooded the fields alongside the road with a silvery light, and the frozen corn stalks left standing in the fields marched along, soldier-like, in a line parallel to the car.

We had been driving about twenty minutes when he turned toward me and said, "We're almost there. A friend of mine owns a large farm, and it has this man-made lake he lets me fish in the summer. And it is a sight to see in the winter."

He turned onto a gravel road and threaded the Jeep through several twists and turns while I held on. In this remote countryside I wondered what could possibly be so spectacular that he would drive miles to see it.

My question was answered as we topped a hill. A small lake lay shimmering in the moonlight. It looked like a large circular urn carefully shaped by some old pagan deity who had filled it to the brim with molten silver.

We got out of the car, and Fleshman flashed a smile at me. "Didn't I tell you?"

He didn't wait for an answer but motioned for me to follow. "Come on, there's more."

I followed behind as he tramped through the snow toward a small pier that jutted out over the lake, my boots crunching the snow and my breath fogging in the icy air.

He stopped at the edge of the pier near a small rough bench and waited for me to catch up. He had brushed the snow from the bench and was standing in front of it. He said, "Now close your eyes and keep them closed until I tell you to turn completely around."

I felt a little foolish, but I did what he said.

"Now. Open your eyes and look."

He was right. It was breath-taking. Etched in black against a wall of white snow was a stand of tall sycamore trees, their barren limbs an intricate web of intersecting lines, black strokes on a white canvas crisscrossed by a master painter.

Above the trees, in the dark sky, the stars looked like chip diamonds flung into space by an exuberant and careless jeweler. It was a living Ansel Adams photograph in stark black and white.

"Ever see anything so beautiful?"

"No," I said, entranced by the scene and the stillness of the moment. It was beautiful enough to push the dirty politics and frustrating disappointment of the day out of my mind. I took a deep breath of the crisp air, dragging it into my lungs and then slowly letting it out.

"The woods are lovely, dark, and deep," he began. He stopped and grinned. "I'm not sure about the next line."

"But I have promises to keep," I added.

"And miles to go before I sleep," he said.

A detective who quotes Frost? Once again I was impressed.

Suddenly a startling sound fragmented the silence. It sounded for all the world like someone yodeling, and it was followed by a kind of strange, startling laughter.

"What in God's name was that?"

He laughed. "Ever hear anything like that before?"

"No," I said.

"It's a loon."

"Loons? In Oklahoma?"

"Yes," he said, laughter in his voice. "At least one loon, and a very peculiar bird he is. He is probably one of a group that migrated south, likely from northern Illinois, going to southern Illinois. But he didn't stop in Illinois. Not this bird. He kept flying southwest until he got to Oklahoma."

"You're making this up."

"I'm not. It's the gospel."

The peculiar sound echoed around us again.

"He'll stay through the winter, but then he'll go back north. Know why?"

"That's what birds do, I guess."

"You're right. Even though he's a daring adventurer, he will go back. And for a very good reason. He has no mate here."

I looked to see if he was serious. He was.

Then I laughed. "You know what, Fleshman, you amaze me. A tough, no-nonsense detective who knows about loons, knows where to find cinematic black and white snow scenes, and can quote at least one line from Robert Frost? I'm impressed."

"That's good. Feeling better?"

I was. I was getting my equilibrium back.

"Want to talk about it? Your bad day?"

"I didn't get the job as dean. Lew Hawkins did."

"I see. That's tough."

I sighed and said. "Yeah, well, I guess that it isn't too surprising that I didn't get it."

"You think this letter, or file, that Munsell thinks you have, and *didn't* give him, made the difference?"

"I think so."

He sat down on the cleared bench and motioned for me to sit beside him. He reached up and took my hand in his. The warmth and strength of his hand as he drew me down beside him comforted me and yet, at the same time, caused a slight tremble of excitement to flow through me.

I looked at him, and he was looking at me. I felt a slight movement of his body toward me, but almost instantly he was consciously pulling himself back.

His face in the moonlight had become serious and constrained. He said, "Look, Connie, I need to talk to you about some things, about the Dean's murder, and Clarence's, I mean."

"Fine," I said, trying to keep the shakiness I was feeling out of my voice.

He ran his hand over his hair, mussing it up. I wondered briefly if that was his attempt to tamp down his emotions, decided it was probably not, and that I was being foolish about the whole thing.

He said, "I need to remind you of again of how necessary it is that you pay attention to where you go and what you do until I am able to find out who killed Dean Stafford. I don't know who that person is yet. Until I do, I want you to be very careful."

I said, "But I am being careful."

"I know. But this last incident, someone trying to run you into a ditch, that's a real threat."

"That could have been a stupid teenager or just a frustrated driver. I don't know if whoever it was meant anything more than to scare me.

And if you are still worried, just remember that I didn't see anything that night, Jake. I just heard footsteps."

"I know." He repeated, "I know. "But I think the murderer is someone who knows you, someone who is watching you."

I said, "And?"

"And I think Clarence finally made the connection between the sailor he thought he saw and the killer. And he was killed to shut him up."

His voice was full of concern. "And if you happen to remember anything, anything at all, that you heard or saw that might expose him, or her, then you must get in touch with me immediately. Will you do that?"

"You can be sure I will, Jake, you can be sure I will."
I meant what I said. I just hoped I would have time, if I remembered anything, to get to him.

Chapter 19

The evening with Fleshman had been a two-edged sword as far as my peace of mind was concerned. On the one hand, the trip to the countryside and the beauty of the evening, along with the momentary warmth of my feeling toward him, had made my disappointment and depression less hurtful, but his continued warning that my life might be in danger hadn't done much to make me less afraid.

To exchange one set of intense emotions for another equally intense one didn't make it easy for me to go to sleep. I tried all the old bromides for relaxing, a soaking, warm bath, meditation to block out negatives, but when I crawled into bed, I remained nervous. Fleshman had said, "I think the murderer is someone who knows you and is watching you." That could be anyone at the University. Because I was Chair of the English department, a lot of people did watch me, either surreptitiously or overtly.

Boyd Finnell was always snooping around, checking on me. Chris Herndon watched me to be able to avoid me, Eddie Parsons flaunted his latest conquest in my face. I was certainly on Nora Tennyson's 'watch list' after she had caught me looking at files in the Dean's office.

But watching me to see if I knew something important about the Dean's murder? Or watching me to see if I had recognized who the murderer was? That was another kind of watching, and that was very disturbing.

My mind kept jumping back to VP Munsell and the reasoning behind his refusal to appoint me as dean. It could not have been because he thought Hawkins would make a better dean. Surely he saw Hawkins for the sycophant and simpleton that he was. But he must have seen me as someone who was consistently defiant of him, refusing to give him the file he was convinced I had. Was he desperate enough to have rummaged through my office, looking for it? I thought, *It could have been him.*

I tossed and turned, weighing the pros and cons of my plan to get a promotion from Munsell. I also listened briefly to what my better voices told me. But I finally came back to my first decision. The only way I could get promoted was to tell Munsell I had the file, and that I would exchange it for a promotion. It was blackmail but it was what I had to do, and the consequences be damned. I'd handle the consequences <u>after</u> I got the promotion.

Nevertheless, it was not a resolution that let me sleep peacefully. Twice I had the dream of being chased by a faceless person in a navy pea coat, brandishing a long sharp dagger, intent on slitting my throat.

Another time it was Aunt Grace, dressed in a gold dress that reflected in a golden light, saying, "It's not right, what you are doing, Connie, it's not right, and you know it." That was not a quiet night, and I woke up tired and listless, wishing that I didn't have to be on campus early for the first day of classes. But I had no choice but to be there for the onslaught of problems that a new semester always provided.

When I got to work, Rosa, my faithful and devoted secretary was in her office, and almost before I put my briefcase down she was handing me a fresh cup of coffee.

"To help your nerves," she said, smiling. She had been through this drill several times with me and knew what a chaotic time it always was. I was grateful for her thoughtfulness. I said, "Thanks, I'll need it."

"It will be crazy," she said, smiling an encouraging smile.

"No doubt about it. Just keep the lines moving, and if I scream, come running."

"Da nada," she said, which, loosely translated meant both "It's nothing fatal," and "you can count on me."

It was twelve thirty before I had a chance to look up from

my desk.   Reassigning students, changing class rooms, and approving course changes had eaten up the morning. I was tired, and I leaned back in my chair, stretching my arms over my head. I was hoping the afternoon would be much quieter.

Nora came to the door and said, "Mrs. Stafford is here and wants to see you." I was completely caught off guard. Why in the world would Helen Stafford want to see me? I nodded to Nora and said, "Tell her to come right in."

Helen paused in the doorway for a second. I hadn't seen her since the Dean's funeral. She was very stylish in a long woolen skirt and an azure shirt. Her silver hair, smooth and sleek, was caught up in a ponytail and pinned with an amber comb.

Even just standing there she was graceful. I sighed. No doubt about it; she was a gorgeous woman. And now, not only was she gorgeous, but she was also wealthy, or she would be when the Dean's insurance paid off.

Could she have murdered him for the money? At that moment, I thought it seemed unlikely. She didn't *look* like a murderer. But then what did I know? What, for heaven's sake, *did* a murderer *look like?*

She moved into the office and said, "Do you have a few minutes, Connie? I need to talk to you. I motioned her toward a chair and said, "Of course." She sat down gracefully across from me.

"Would you like a cup of coffee," I asked

She smiled. "No thank you. I won't take much of your time. I just need to say something to you that has been bothering me."

My first thought was that whatever she had to say might not be very pleasant. I shifted in my chair and said, "Go right ahead, Helen."

"I want to apologize for the rude and thoughtless way I spoke to you the night you and the Detective came to my house. I was drunk and your message was a total shock to me, but I had no reason to be ugly to you and the Detective."

She sounded honest and contrite, but I was surprised. Helen was not known for being apologetic. I stumbled a bit but managed to say, "It was a shock, I know, and hearing it so bluntly must have very difficult. I understand."

I did understand, I think, but I was still wary.

She looked at me thoughtfully, and then said, "Would you tell Detective Fleshman that I regret how I treated him?" She reached her hand toward me, as if she were appealing in some subliminal way to my understanding of her distress, but quickly drew it back.

For a moment, I just sat there, nonplussed. How should I respond? Tell her she needed to tell Fleshman herself? Or should I take her distress as real and do my best to help her by doing as she asked?

I could certainly imagine her not wanting to talk to Fleshman in person. He had the formidable ability to make you feel guilty whether you were or not. I hesitated for a long minute, then, hoping that I was not being deceived and manipulated I said, "I'll be glad to tell him, Helen. I know this whole thing has been terribly difficult for you."

She seemed genuinely grateful for my response. Her smile was warm and engaging. She said, "I do appreciate this, Connie, more than you know."

She stood up and this time reached out her hand to me. I shook it, and she turned and left. I hurriedly gathered my book and lecture notes and headed for my next class.

The class was made up of former students, and, by and large, they were bright and eager learners. They were the kind of students who made the academic life worthwhile. The rest of it, the politics, the meaningless committee meetings, the petty, egotistical professors I had to deal with was nothing but fluff.

I was fifteen minutes into my opening lecture on Hamlet when I glimpsed Rosa standing outside the door, looking distressed.

Knowing that she would never interrupt a class unless it were an emergency, I stepped outside and said, "What is it, Rosa?"

She glanced nervously up and down the hallway and then back to me. "It's Dr. Finnell's class. He's not there and the students are making so much noise the other professors are complaining."

"Have you checked to see if he's in his office?"

"He's not there. I can't find him anywhere."

"Okay, I'll take care of it. Wait in the office in case he calls." I went back into my class, finished my short introduction, and dismissed them.

Then I hurried toward the second floor and Finnell's classroom. What could have happened to him? He never missed a class. It was one of his few virtues, an obsession almost. He bragged about his attendance record like a first grader brags about getting a gold star.

The only logical explanation for his absence must be that he was ill. But why didn't he call in?

When I got to his classroom, the hubbub had died down. Only a handful of the athletes who made up the bulk of his class remained. I dismissed them, promising that Finnell would be back in class on Wednesday.

Then I spied Aloysius Jones, slumped in a chair at the back of the room. He waited a second, then straightened up and said, "I don't think Professor Finnell will be back Wednesday. I think he's gone."

He looked uncomfortable and his eyes darted nervously around the empty room. He glanced at the doorway as if he might break and run. I moved to block the door in case he did and said, "What do you mean, you think he's gone? Gone where?"

"I don't know." His voice had taken on a whine, and he kept his head down with his eyes focused on his feet. He's just gone. I went by his house Saturday and Sunday, and he wasn't there."

"You warned him, didn't you, Aloysius? In spite of what I said? You told him his alibi was no good."

His head jerked up. His eyes were frightened and panic spread over his face. I wanted to shake him until his eyes popped.

He had warned Finnell that I had said that his alibi was full of holes. And now Finnell was gone, God only knew where. I smothered my damn and said, "That was a stupid thing to do."

He whined, "I don't want Prof Finnell to get in no trouble."

"Then if you have any idea where he might be, it would be smart for you to get in touch with him. Tell him to call me. Do you understand that, Aloysius?"

He nodded. He was beginning to sweat.

I had succeeded in scaring him, and I pushed a little harder. "And if you tell anyone else about any of this, I promise you will be in more trouble than you can imagine."

He looked miserable as he slid by me.

When I got back to the office, my first impulse was to call Fleshman, but when I calmed down, I had second thoughts. I needed to try and find Finnell on my own.

First, I would check his house, being very careful about that. If he were really sick and caught me checking on him, he would be furious. His reaction to things was never normal. His paranoia was always simmering just below the surface and it would take very little for him to explode.

It was around three thirty before the last student cleared out of my office. It had been a typically horrendous first day, and I was tired, but I determined to drive by Finnell's house before I went home. He hadn't answered his phone all day.

When I got into the area, I drove slowly by the house, but there was no sign of life. The garage door was closed and the house looked empty. I circled the block and came back, and then stopped across the street under some trees.

Parked there in the shadows, I felt foolish, like someone in a B movie. I slumped down in the seat, making myself as inconspicuous as possible and hoping no one would see me.

I waited what seemed to be an interminable time, thinking that if this was what real detectives did it was not much fun. The wind had picked up and the temperature was plummeting. The heavy clouds looked as if they might drop snow any minute. I was getting cold, even with the heater on so I decided to do what I had come to do.

I got out of the car, walked to the front door and rang the bell, stomping my feet to keep off the chill. There was no answer. I hadn't thought there would be.

I went around the side of the garage and peered in through the window. His car was gone so I decided that I had done enough detecting for one day.

Shivering from both the cold and a growing conviction that Finnell had skipped out of town, I ran back to the car and jumped in. I wanted to go home, take a hot bath, and get something in my empty stomach.

On the way home I deliberated about calling Fleshman but decided not to. If Finnell missed his Wednesday classes, that would be time enough to get the police involved.

At home, I got warm, ate a small pizza, and went into the den to listen to the TV for thirty minutes. The news was boring so I turned it off.

The fire in the fireplace was comforting and I sat there, mindless and unthinking, for fifteen minutes. Then I realized how tired I was from the rigors of the day.

I stretched, yawned, and headed for my bedroom. I quickly undressed and fell, exhausted, into bed. I was asleep in another fifteen minutes.

Sometime later I abruptly awoke from a sound sleep. I sat up in bed, wide-eyed, my heart racing. A nameless fear swept over me. Something was wrong. I glanced at the bay window, Tess's sleeping place. She was standing there, a dark statue, her eyes focused on the blackness outside the window.

"Tess," I whispered. She didn't move. Then I heard it. A faint, crunching sound, like the careful placing of a foot in the icy snow. Then another step. *Someone was outside my window.*

A numbing fear paralyzed me. The blood thundered in my ears, and my hands shook. I made no attempt to pick up the phone by my bed. It didn't seem to be an option. Whoever was there could get inside and kill me before I could get any help.

By the faint light in my room, I saw flakes of snow hitting the window, but I was immobilized, afraid to move. I was trapped and helpless inside my own bedroom.

Then Tess turned away from the window, her eyes

flashing in the half light of the room. She meowed, a plaintive mewling sound, and jumped on the bed.

Her movement triggered a reaction in me. I lunged off the bed, jerked the drapes closed, and leaned against the window, my breath coming in quick shallow bursts. The closed drapes, a kind of barrier, gave me some comfort.

I slid down on the floor and sat there for at least another three minutes until my heart slowed and my mind began to focus more clearly. I took several deep, calming breaths while I decided what to do. Whoever had been outside had seen the drapes being pulled and that might have scared him off. But I couldn't be sure.

I had to do something. For the first time in my life, I wished I had a gun.

My eyes had adjusted to the darkened room, and I could see fairly well. Hunkering down, I crawled away from the window to the doorway, opened the door, and quickly slipped into the hallway. I didn't turn on the lights. The darkness was my ally.

I managed to get to the kitchen without knocking anything over, and I could see the entire backyard through the kitchen window.

I didn't see anyone, and I began to breathe easier. I still didn't turn on any lights, but the pale moonlight filtering through the windows gave me enough light to look around. The clock showed that it was three a.m.

I decided I would stand up and move to the kitchen table. I sat there, wishing desperately for a cup of coffee to steady my hands.

Then Tess ambled into the room looking for me. "You did good, Tess," I whispered, "You're a great watch-cat, and scared the bad guy off."

I was talking to bolster my courage more than anything else, but Tess seemed to understand. I patted her head, and said, "Let's go into the den."

I walked cautiously down the hall. I was glad that I had left the fireplace on. I had no desire to go back to my bedroom. I sat staring into the fire, thinking of how drastically my life had changed in the brief time since Stafford's death.

My colleagues and I had suddenly become suspects in a double murder. For some reason, I had become the target of a threatening email letter. Then someone had tried to run me off the road, maybe accidentally, maybe not, and now someone was stalking me at home.

More than that, my career wasn't going anywhere. Munsell had seen to that, and I was scheming to get even with him. To top it all, I had a new Dean to deal with, someone I had no respect for.

The only good thing that had happened in all of this chaos was that I had met an intelligent and capable police lieutenant whom I liked and respected. I was convinced he wouldn't give up until he found who murdered Stafford and Clarence. For that I was thankful.

My mind went back to dear Matt, and I remembered, gratefully, that he had promised me a trip to San Diego very soon. I finally fell asleep on the couch, thinking about lying on the beach in the bright California sunshine while cool winds came in from the ocean and caressed my face.

Chapter 20

When I awoke, the early morning daylight was filtering into the den, and I glanced at my watch, afraid that I had overslept. I hadn't. It was only seven o'clock.

I yawned and stretched. Sleeping on the couch had not been restful. My back was aching and my eyes felt grainy and heavy. I needed a coffee transfusion, but my first priority was to check for footprints outside my bedroom window.

I pulled on jeans, sweater, and boots and hurried out. The sky was overcast from the heavy snow of last night and the backyard lay under a pristine coat of white.

I glanced around the fenced backyard, looking for a path that an intruder might have made, but the deep snow was smooth and unmarred. It was my guess that he had come up from the small creek bed behind my house. I checked the gate. It was latched, but it didn't have a lock on it, so it could have been opened from outside.

I walked carefully to the bedroom window and knelt in the snow. I could see slight indentations that could have been footprints, but the new snow had effectively obscured them. I brushed the snow aside, hoping that there would be something, but there was no clear pattern.

It would be impossible to prove that anyone had been outside the window, but *I knew* that someone had been there. I went inside and made coffee, anxious for the warmth and the jolt of the caffeine that would chase the nightmarish thoughts away. I wanted to call Fleshman, but it was too early. He wouldn't be at work, and I hesitated to call him at home.

But I could call Matt. He might be grumpy, but he would listen and he might offer to come over. I dialed his phone. He answered on the third ring, and his voice was cheery.

"You've been up awhile," I said.

"Since six a.m. I took a long walk, stretched my muscles and breathed in a lot of clean, fresh air. It's a great day to be outside. Why are you up so early?"

"I had a little detective work to do, but it didn't pan out."

"What're you talking about?" The lilt had gone from his voice.

"I was checking out my back yard because someone had been prowling around last night. Someone was outside my window, and it scared me."

"I spent most of the night huddled in the den with Tess. I finally fell asleep an hour or so before dawn."

"Damn it, Con, are you all right?"

"I'm frazzled from lack of sleep and I'm a bit nervous, but I'm okay."

"I'm coming over. I'll stop by a deli and bring breakfast. Wait for me."

I felt better. I always did after I talked to Matt.

Hurriedly I jumped into the shower, and I barely had time to get into my clothes when the doorbell rang.

I went to the door, carefully checked the peep hole before I opened it. I wondered if I would ever throw open a door again without checking first to see who was there, knew I wouldn't. A damn night prowler had effectively made a coward out of me.

Matt, looking anxious and carrying a deli package in his hand pushed inside. His first words were, "Are you all right?"

"I'm okay. As I said, a little nervous, but okay." I pointed him toward the kitchen. "I'll tell you all about it, but right now I've got to dry my hair. Wait here. I'll be back in five minutes."

He said, "First, I'm going outside to check things out." He handed me the package and was gone before I could protest.

When I finished drying my hair, I went back to the kitchen. He was still outside, plowing around in the snow.

I was pretty sure he wouldn't find anything, but I didn't bother him. I popped the omelets into the microwave and heated the English muffins, glancing occasionally at him through the kitchen window.

I saw him open the gate and disappear from sight. He had apparently had the same thought I had and was checking around the creek bed. Finally he came back, stopping on the patio to stomp the snow from his feet.

Coming into the room, he answered the question he saw in my eyes. "I didn't find anything, but it's easy enough to get inside your backyard without being seen. The trees and bushes along the creek bank are convenient places to hide."

"Thanks for looking around, I said and hugged him. He hugged me back, and then held me at arm's length. He had a frown on his face. "I don't like you meddling in this murder investigation. Why don't you let it go? Let Fleshman do his thing."

I said, "I would have, if it had just been the Dean who was killed. I know that sounds callous, but Clarence was a victim also. And that makes it imperative that this murderer be caught and punished."

My voice was getting shrill. I took a deep breath. I was still tired, and I didn't need to get emotionally stirred up again.

Matt, always sensitive to my moods, said, "Okay. Okay." He grinned. "Let's eat and talk about something else.

When we sat down and I began to eat, I realized I was famished. Between bites, I said, "How is Annette? Have you been to see her lately?"

"I flew up Saturday, came back Sunday. She's okay. She is busy getting ready for her last semester at Holyoke."

"When is she coming for a visit? I haven't seen her in ages."

"Don't think she will. She's leaving for Paris right after graduation. She wants to spend a year there, seeing the sights, doing nothing in particular. Then she will decide where she wants to do graduate work."

"Maybe the next time I can go with you, Matt. I've always adored Annette."

"I probably won't go back before she leaves. He smiled and said, "Annette always asks how you are."

He poured himself another cup of coffee, stirred cream and sugar in, took a sip, and looked at me. This time *his* eyes were questioning.

"What?" I said.

"Want to talk about Hawkins?"

I felt my face flush, and I looked down at my coffee cup. Matt had heard that I had been passed over and Hawkins promoted.

Everyone at the University knew it by now, were talking about it, and probably some of them were feeling sorry for me.

I hated that. I didn't want anyone's pity. I said, "What's to tell? Hawkins got the job; I didn't."

"It's a damn shame. We both know it was political. You're hands down ten times better dean material than Hawkins."

I had to smile. Matt's unequivocal defense of me was heartwarming. He had always been supportive of my ambition to get ahead.

I said, "You're absolutely right, I'd have been a much better dean. What can I say?"

We both laughed.

"One more thing," he said, his voice becoming sober. "I'm getting you a gun, and I'm teaching you how to use it."

"To shoot Hawkins? I think that's a great idea."

In spite of himself, he smiled. "I'm serious, either get a gun, or I move in with you."

"Moving in would cause some talk, don't you think?

I said, "Look, I can always call on Aunt Grace if I need to. She loves spending the night. And I promise I'll do that. But no gun."

I thought he was going to argue, but instead he reached out and took my hand, "You are something else, you know that?"

I nodded and smiled. Then I said, "Thanks for coming over, Matt. Thanks for the food. And now I've got to get rid of you so I can go to work.

I reached up and hugged him, placed a kiss on his cheek. I said, "You are my best friend and I love you. You know that."

"And I love you, my dear Connie. and someday I'm going to take you away from all this."

He walked to the door, paused, and with his eyes twinkling, said, "I am your knight in shining armor, look for me on my white horse almost any day."

Chapter 21

By the time I got to the university, the previous scary night had begun to fade from my mind because of other pressing problems. I had a note on my desk that Dean Hawkins wanted to see me sometime when I was free. Seeing his name with "Dean" before it for the first time forced me into a reality check. He was Dean, and I would have to accept that fact, no matter how distasteful it was.

I had a pretty good idea what he wanted to talk to me about. By now he had seen all the classes and assignments for the new semester. And no doubt he had seen the special schedule that Helen Stafford had been given.

I had long ago given up trying to make her class load conform to the norm because of her special dispensation from Dean Stafford. The regular teaching load was four classes. She only taught one class. The rest of her teaching load was time was set for her to advise the students who were taking her class, a feature that no other professor had.

I assumed that the new Dean had seen the discrepancy and had determined to make drastic changes in her schedule. I couldn't repress a grin as I thought of Hawkins tangling with her.

Helen was smarter than he was and even without the support of her dead husband, I would bet money that she had been the winner in her confrontation with the newly elected Dean Hawkins.

I deliberately did not go to his office until the middle of the afternoon. I had waited until two-thirty to check Finnell's class, hoping that he would be there with a reasonable explanation of his earlier absence. But he did not show, and I knew I would have to tell Hawkins.

The students had cleared out and the building filled up with the peculiar quiet and peacefulness that follows their exodus. I fortified myself for the meeting with a cup of coffee and walked slowly toward Hawkin's office.

I remembered how I had walked the same hallway to the Dean's office a short few weeks ago with *two* cups in my hand, and what I had found that night.

In the silence of the hallway I heard my heels clicking in a slow, studied rhythm. I had deliberately slowed my pace because I was in no hurry to harangue with Hawkins.

It was then that a light turned on in my mind. I stopped dead in my tracks. The footsteps I had heard that night. . . there had been a pattern to them! The person had been walking fast, but there was a click and a slap, a click and a slap, a click and a slap, all the way down the hallway. "

That's it," I said aloud. "That's it."

Something had been nagging at me about that Sunday night for days, but I had not been able to pin it down. Until this moment I had not been able to dredge it up out of my subconscious and make the connection.

My heart was ripping along at cardiac-arrest speed, and my hand holding my cup was shaking so badly that the coffee was sloshing onto the floor.

It took me several minutes before I could quiet down enough to think lucidly or act normally. I dropped to one of the benches lining the hall and sat there a moment collecting my senses.

Then another chilling thought flashed into my mind. The murderer of Stafford and Clarence is someone I know, and he is afraid that I will recognize who he is.

That is why the warning email. Perhaps he was the one in the car who was trying to force me off the road. Maybe he was the night prowler.

These thoughts rattled around in my brain, forcing me to action. I stood up. Someone who walked with that particular gait might be recognizable by the gait itself *if someone were intent on listening.*

I recognized that it was a tenuous piece of evidence at best, and that it might be difficult to prove anything with it,

.

But it might be enough to frighten a nervous murderer into making some kind of mistake if the idea was floated out into the open. At any rate, it was worth mentioning to Fleshman when I saw him again.

Hawkins' secretary was Nora, who had worked for Dean Stafford, and apparently intended to keep the position.

She barely looked up from her computer when I entered her office. Wordlessly she motioned me toward Hawkins' open door, and I stepped inside.

Hawkins was perched behind Stafford's massive desk and looked like a timid bird sitting in a lion's seat. Apparently he had decided that as dean he needed to dress to impress, and he had substituted his usual shabby corduroy jacket and baggy trousers for a navy blue double breasted suit, white shirt, and regimental striped red tie.

To me, he succeeded in looking like an uncomfortable trained monkey. The only thing missing was the tin cup.

He got right to the point. "I've had a request from Helen Stafford to keep her one class to a minimum of ten students, and give her six additional hours credit which will provide her with advisement time for those ten students. His face was a question mark.

"That's her usual schedule," I said.

"Why does she only teach one class when everyone else teaches four? And why is she paid for a full load for teaching one class and 'advising students time?' How can that be?"

Looking at me suspiciously, he added. "Why such a ridiculous schedule for Helen Stafford?"

I said, "Because her teaching load was assigned by Dean Stafford. He approved her special schedule."

His eyebrows shot up, and his slicked down hair sprang out in spiky tufts, making him look more like a monkey than ever.

His voice was sharp. "That practice will stop. I don't have any intention of giving her paid time for advisement of students. She can do her advisement just as everybody else does, on their own free time."

I tried not to smile. I could see Helen's eyes turn to blue fire when Hawkins told her that her schedule would be changed so drastically.

Helen was not someone he could jerk around very easily. She undoubtedly had school connections that reached to the President's office and beyond to the Board of Regents.

But I was not about to tell him any of that.

He would certainly learn the hard way. I just nodded and said, "That's fine with me. You are the Dean."

I stood up and said, "And now I need to get back to my office; work is piling up on my desk."

I moved quickly to the door, not giving him a chance to stop me. I was out of his office and halfway down the hall before I realized I hadn't told him about Finnell.

But to my mind, Hawkins didn't really need to know about Finnell. My first priority was to get in touch with Fleshman.

I needed to tell him about Finnell being gone, but more importantly, I needed to tell him about recognizing the sound pattern of the footsteps that Sunday night. He might think that it was something significant.

Chapter 22

When I got back to my office, Rosa, my secretary, was gone, but she had left two messages. Aloysius Jones had come by to ask if Dr. Finnell was back, and Detective Fleshman had returned my call. I could barely contain my nervousness as I dialed Fleshman's number.

He said, "Hey, I was about to call you,"

I said, "And I've got some news for you."

"I'm listening."

Pleased and more than a little proud that I had recognized a pattern to the footsteps, I told him that I thought it might be a good clue.

But apparently he was not impressed. His "Hummm..." was not the enthusiastic response I had expected. A little crestfallen, I said, "You don't sound too excited. It was a real breakthrough for me. It put to rest a nagging at my consciousness that had been worrying me."

"It's something, sure. But did you recognize who it was?"

I said, "No, but it makes me think it is someone I know, and maybe sooner or later I'll make that connection."

"That will be good," he said, "if you can. But if you do, it will still be difficult to prove. The problem is that it is not solid evidence."

He smiled and said, "I mean, I can't arrest someone just because he walks funny."

I felt my hackles rising. I said, a little tartly, "Can't put too much reliance on a woman's sudden insight, is that it? Well, just to let you know that someone out there is getting nervous about what I might or might not know, I had a prowler outside my window last evening."

That got his attention.

He wanted details, and I elaborated on the whole frightening scene for him. But when I got to the part about Matt and me scouring the area the next morning, he interrupted, and sounded a bit irritated. "

"You shouldn't have done that. Now there's no chance of my people finding anything."

"Sorry. But at the time it seemed the right thing to do."

I didn't like being chided for doing the most natural thing in the world -- looking for footprints where someone had been lollygagging under my window. And if there had been anything to find, either Matt or I would have found it.

"Okay. Any idea who it might have been?"

"Not for sure." I paused a second before I added, "But Boyd Finnell has disappeared. He hasn't been to class for two days, hasn't been at his regular eating places, and he's not at home."

"Is this unusual for him?"

"He never misses classes. It's a point of pride with him."

"Any other reason for him to do something like this?"

'I am not absolutely sure. But Aloysius Jones and his girlfriend, who were supposed to have been with him all that evening, came in and confessed that they had left him alone at the basketball game for at least an hour."

I paused. "Which seems to me to shoot a pretty big hole in his alibi."

"Do you have any idea where he might be now? What about relatives?"

"No idea where he might be. He was always tight lipped about his personal business. The only relative he ever mentioned was a sister who lives in Nashville. Her name is Ophelia Box. I remember her name because I thought it was unusual."

"Could it have been Finnell at your window?"

"I don't know. Maybe. Unless he's out of town."

"Okay. I'll contact the police in Nashville, and have them check out this Ophelia Box to see if Finnell might be there. And I will l have a police car cruising your neighborhood at night."

"If your night visitor was a one-time burglar, he probably won't be back, but I don't want to take any chances. If Finnell turns up, call me."

I was disappointed when he hung up. He hadn't seemed terribly thrilled about any of the information I'd given him. I sat staring at the phone for several seconds.

Then an idea popped into my mind. Why not put my own analytical skills to work? After all, I had been trained to think critically. I could dissect a Shakespearean sonnet, analyze T.S. Eliot's Wasteland, and make sense out of a novel by Thomas Hardy. Why not figure out a scenario for murder? Or at least study the cast?

I turned to my trusty computer. I lined up four columns: name, motive, opportunity, alibi. Under names I wrote Boyd Finnell, Nora Tennyson, Chris Herndon, Helen Stafford, Eddie Parsons, VP Munsell, and Lew Hawkins.

I hesitated a moment then added Matt's name along with mine. I felt a little silly doing it, but to be objective I had to put down everyone Fleshman had interviewed as a possible suspect.

The motive column was easy to fill out. Everyone on the list had reason to hate Stafford, including me.

I was checking the opportunity column, filling in a yes or no, when I sensed that someone was standing in the doorway.

Frightened, I turned quickly. It was Aunt Grace. I clutched my hands over my chest and said, "My God, Aunt Grace, you scared the hell out of me!" My outburst rattled her so much she didn't think to chastise me for swearing.

She said, "My goodness, I'm sorry. I thought you heard me. I stopped by to get you out of this office and take you to dinner."

Immediately I was contrite. "Sit down Aunt Grace. Sorry I jumped at you."

"You really are nervous, Constance. What's bothering you?"

For a second, I thought about telling her about my night prowler, but I decided to wait until we were at a restaurant where she wouldn't make too much fuss about it.

I smiled and said, "It's just that I was deep in a little

detective work, and I didn't expect you."

The mention of detective work piqued her interest. I knew it would. Her blue eyes sparkled. "Can I help? I love mysteries, and I'm good at figuring out who the guilty person is. Before the end of the book."

"Why not?" I said. "You know everybody on this list; I've fussed about them often enough."

I hit the print button, ran off two copies of my suspect sheet, and handed one to her. I added, "Everyone had reason to hate Stafford, and probably, at one time or another, wanted to kill him. Question is who went over the edge and did it."

She looked up. "For heaven's sake, why did you put down your name -- and Matt's?"

"Well, an outsider making a suspect list would put our names down. Matt has had run-ins with Stafford, and there have been times when I would have killed the Dean if I'd had the nerve. And we're both part of the scene."

Aunt Grace's face told me she had quickly discredited *that* answer, and she had already focused her attention back on the list. "You've written down a motive for everyone. I need to ask some questions."

"Go ahead." It was as good a way as any to get another perspective, and Aunt Grace was no dummy. She was stubborn, contentious, and arrogantly self-confident, but her mind was razor sharp.

She said, "Beside Helen Stafford's name you've written *money*. How much money are we talking about?"

"She will get half a million from his insurance policy."

She scribbled something by Helen's name, and then said, "What does this mean: Finnell, paranoid bombshell. Ran away?"

"Finnell hated Stafford, had an abnormal fear that he was looking for ways to get rid of him. And Finnell has disappeared. Apparently, he left town when his alibi collapsed."

"A suspicious move for sure." Her finger moved down the list again. What about these next two, Herndon and Parsons. You've written *going to be fired by Stafford.* Why?"

"I've told you about Chris Herndon and his problem with alcohol. He's been getting worse, showing up in class drunk more and more often. Fleshman found a file on him in Stafford's home. The Dean had given him an ultimatum. If he showed up drunk in class one more time, he would be terminated.

As for Eddie Parsons, he is being sued for sexual harassment by a graduate student. The Dean was going to testify against him."

"So either of these men might have been desperate enough to kill?"

I shrugged. "I don't know, Aunt Grace. It is possible."

"These are not good people you are working with, Constance." She said it so solemnly that I had to laugh.

"You're absolutely right, Aunt Grace. They *are not* good country people."

She was back at the list. "Who is Munsell and why a question mark by his name?"

"He is Vice President of Financial and Academic Affairs. The question mark is because there was something between him and Stafford, a strong tie of some kind, but I don't know what it was."

"What does he have to do with financial affairs? Does that mean he handles University money?"

"He's an overseer of it all, and he's in charge of money that comes in as gifts for the University."

"Then there's a money angle that needs investigating."

"Detective Fleshman is checking on that now."

She pointed at the next name. "Is this Hawkins the one who politicked his way into the job you should have had? The new Dean?" Her voice was edged with anger.

"The same," I said.

"You can mark him off the list, Constance. A man who grovels and fawns his way up the ladder is not a passionate man, and this murderer is someone moved by a deep passion."

She glanced at the list again. "But why is Nora Tennyson on the list? You've told me how loyal she was to the Dean, how she covered up for him. And why 'enigma' beside her name?"

"Because there's something puzzling about Nora. She was loyal to Stafford, and she turned down excellent job offers to stay with him. I have often wondered why."

"Maybe she was in love with him? It happens, you know."

"I don't think so, but what do I know? It's hard to figure why people do what they do. Maybe she stayed simply because she liked being personal secretary to the Dean."

She looked at me thoughtfully and said, "Give me a few minutes. I need to think through this list again."

I was smart enough to know that I should sit back and shut up. Looking at my copy of the suspect list, I continued to check yes or no in the opportunity column, but out of the corner of my eye, I watched her.

She scribbled furiously, stopping at intervals to chew on her pencil and look off into the distance as if she was waiting for some kind of divine revelation.

Finally, after thirty minutes or more had gone by, she said, "All right. That's it. You want to know what I make of this suspect list?"

I said, "Yes," wondering if she would pick Finnell.

Her answer surprised me. "I think the murder of the Dean had to do with money."

She saw the surprise on my face and said, "Think with me, Constance. With five of these people, money played an important part in their relationship to Dean Stafford.

The Dean's death would insure certain things: Helen Stafford would become wealthy. Chris Herndon and Eddie Parsons would have the threat of losing their jobs gone, and the money they make. Nora Tennyson would be free to find a more lucrative job. And with Vice President Munsell, I'd bet that his connection with the Dean had to do with money, got legally or otherwise."

"But what about Hawkins and Finnell? Why eliminate them?"

"Because Hawkins is a worm who hasn't the courage to kill anyone. Finnell is paranoid, but he is also a bully. He's like one of my seventh graders who talked big, but crumbled when someone called his hand. Finnell ran like the coward he is. He's not your murderer."

"But money as a motive for murder?"

The idea surprised me. Then I remembered the Dean's expensive tastes: his elegant suits, his Mercedes, his expensive condo, his squiring of the rich society women of Oklahoma City. His salary wouldn't support such a lifestyle.

"Well?" said Aunt Grace.

"I don't know."

"The Good Book says, 'the love of money is the root of all evil.'"

"But what about Clarence? Certainly no one would profit from his death."

"Clarence found out something about the killer, probably knew who he was. That's why he was killed."

I was dumbfounded. Aunt Grace had come to the same conclusion about Clarence that Fleshman had.

"Tell your detective to follow the money trail, Constance. That is how he'll find the murderer."

Chapter 23

Driving home from dinner with Aunt Grace, I praised myself for being able to dissuade her from spending the night with me. After I told her about the prowler, making it seem as non-threatening as possible, she was intent on staying with me for as long as was necessary. That meant an indefinite time, and I knew that such prolonged togetherness would drive both of us to the edge of insanity.

What finally convinced her that she didn't need to stay with me was telling her that Fleshman had dispatched police cars to cruise by my house all night.

I'm sure she pictured him as being in the patrol car most of the time, and I was also confident that she would be calling him to find out just exactly how many times the cars patrolled.

It was dark when I pulled into the driveway. I punched the garage door opener, grateful for the magic of modern technology which turned on brilliant lights and eliminated any chance of someone lurking unseen in the garage.

I sat in the car, doors locked, until the door came down and secured the area. Then I hurried inside.

I was late and I was sure Tess would be at the door, waiting either to pounce on me or give me one of her go-to-hell looks. I threw my briefcase on the kitchen table and cautiously approached the kitchen stove.

If she was angry enough, that's where she would be. She wasn't there. I was relieved to get safely past that point of attack.

I hurried to the den, opened the door and reached for the light switch.

The door slammed shut, and someone grabbed me from behind, twisting my arm painfully and jerking me close to him. His breath was hot on my neck and he hissed, "Don't scream. This is a gun in your back."

I heard Tess meowing from the den closet. My heart was in my throat. I recognized the voice. It was Boyd Finnell.

He said, "If I let you go, will you be quiet? I don't want to hurt you, but I will if you start screaming."

I could smell his fear. My stomach muscles tightened and I willed my voice to be steady. "I won't scream," I said.

He released my arm and pushed me away from him, still pointing the gun at me. His hand holding the gun was trembling, and his eyes were wild looking.

The thought raced through my mind that he might be on drugs. I scarcely dared breathe.

He looked as if he had slept in his clothes. A heavy mackinaw hung loosely over his suit coat. His forehead was beaded with sweat. I managed to say, "What are you doing here, Finnell?"

He motioned me further into the room, waving the gun. "Turn on the fireplace," he said, "I'm freezing."

My own hands were shaking so that it took me three attempts to snap the fireplace lighter on and get the fire started.

When I turned toward him, he said, "Pull a chair up close to the fireplace. You sit on the couch."

I watched him sink into the winged back chair I had edged close to the fireplace. He shifted the gun to his left hand, held out his right hand toward the fire and said, "It's cold."

The hysteria that edged his voice frightened me, but I kept my voice calm. "What are you doing here? What do you want?"

"Police cars circle your house every forty minutes. Did you know that?" He had a self-satisfied smile on his face that made me grit my teeth.

"You have been checking?" I asked, deciding that the best thing I could do was to keep him talking. He might relax enough to lower the gun. It was frightening to see him waving it around as he had been doing.

He said, "They're looking for a prowler, but they're not very smart. They didn't check the trees along the creek side."

I made the connection. "It was you, wasn't it? Outside last night?"

He smiled a satisfied smile, and said, "I decided it would be easy to come in through the back door tonight. No bright lights out there."

There will be, I thought. *If I get out of this, my whole place will be lit up like a Christmas tree.*

"Why not put the gun down?" I cautiously suggested.

"I'll get coffee for us and you can tell me where you've been. All your students are worried about you."

There was a slight change in his expression. The mention of his students worrying about him appealed to his ego, as I knew it would. He had bought into the concern I had forced into my voice.

He slid the gun into his coat pocket and followed me into the kitchen, watching me carefully as I microwaved two cups of breakfast coffee.

When we walked back into the den, I heard Tess meowing. Knowing how she hated to be cooped up, I said, "Can I please let my cat out of the closet?"

That was a mistake. His face clouded up. "Not on your life; that cat's a demon."

Tess had probably attacked him. I wondered if he had hurt her. I decided I had better change the subject. "

Do you want to tell me where you've been? Your students are upset because you've missed two class days."

He took a sip of his coffee. "I fooled everybody, didn't I? Best place to hide is in plain sight. I've been at Lake Tenkiller in an empty cabin. Just thirty minutes from here."

"Why did you run?"

"Don't be stupid, Crashaw. You know why. I'm the Number One Suspect. When Aloysius gave me up, I knew Fleshman would come after me for Stafford's murder."

His voice went up a decibel and he added, "And I didn't kill him. I didn't kill Clarence. I didn't kill anybody."

"Okay. Okay," I said, making my voice as soothing as possible. "Why don't you tell me why you came here tonight?"

He stood up suddenly and began to pace in front of the fireplace, running his hand nervously through his hair. Finally he stopped and planted himself in front of me. "I need for you to listen to me, and then make my case to that detective."

"I'm listening."

"I didn't kill the dean, but I was in his office earlier that night." He paused, watching for my reaction.

I kept a straight face and said, "All right. So?"

"The Dean had put a note in my mailbox on Friday. I was to be in his office at seven p.m. sharp on Sunday. He didn't say why, just said I was to be there."

His face flushed. "I didn't get there until seven thirty. I wasn't going to let him push me around like I was a peon. When I got to his office, he was sitting behind his big desk like some kind of judge. He stared at me like I was a bug he needed to squash.

"I asked him what he wanted, and he threw a report across the desk. A black woman in my class claimed I had harassed her and given her an unfair grade. Said her lawyer would sue if I didn't apologize and change the grade.

I told him to forget it, I wasn't changing any grade. He was furious. Threatened to write up a reprimand and make it a permanent part of my file. I told him if he did I would sue him for defamation of character.

He came around the desk, punched his finger in my chest like I was some high school kid and said, 'You're a paranoid bastard, Finnell.'

"I swung at him and missed, but I hit the desk and skinned my knuckle. He backed off, grabbed the phone and waved it at me. He said, "Get out, or I'll call the campus police."

I got out, and when I calmed down, I went to the basketball game. That's the God's truth.

I didn't kill Stafford." His voice had lost its fire, and he was looking more and more like a homeless person who had wandered in off the street. His eyes were dull and his shoulders sagged. I said, "The smart thing for you to do is come back to school, get your classes in order, and then go and tell Detective Fleshman what you've told me."

"Do you believe me?"

"Yes," I said. Strangely enough, I did. He was a coward and a contemptible human being, but I didn't think he was a murderer. As Aunt Grace had expressed it, he was a paranoid bully, not a killer.

I held out my hand. "Give me the gun, and let me call Detective Fleshman. You can explain this to him. He's a reasonable man."

He stared at me, his eyes flat and expressionless, and I wondered if I had said the right thing. It seemed an interminable time before he moved, but when he did. he slumped down in the chair near the fireplace, looked up at me and said, "Call him."

"First, the gun." I held out my hand again, surprised that it was steady. My insides were like jelly.

He reached into his waistband and handed it to me, butt forward, a slight frown creasing his face. I reached for it cautiously. I had no knowledge of guns and I was afraid it might go off.

He said, "It's not loaded. I don't know how to handle a gun, so I didn't load it."

I picked up the phone and dialed the police station, wondering what I would do if Fleshman wasn't there. Thankfully he was.

Finnell and I sipped on coffee and carefully avoided looking each other in the eye for the twenty minutes it took Fleshman to get there.

When the doorbell rang, I glanced at Finnell, still apprehensive of what he might do, but he didn't move.

When I opened the door, Jake said, "Where is he? Are you all right?"

I pointed toward the den and said, "I'm fine." Which was not true. All the tension had run out of me like water out of a spigot, leaving me feeling weak.

I said, "Finnell is in the den. His gun is on the desk. But it isn't loaded."

He moved quickly into the den and picked up the gun. He checked it and put it in his coat pocket before he sat down across from Finnell.

Then he said, "You want to tell me what's going on? Why you skipped out of town, came back and broke in here with a gun?"

Finnell avoided his eyes and looked down at his shoes. His voice was quiet but truculent.

He said, "I figured I was your chief suspect. When Aloysius told me he wasn't going to back me up, I panicked. The worst thing was I *had been* in the Dean's office that night, and I knew you'd find out."

"You'd better tell me about that."

Finnell repeated what he had told me.

When he finished, a little of his old defiance surfaced. "I didn't kill the Dean. I didn't harass that black woman either, but Stafford didn't believe me. He was going to *punish me* for something I didn't do. I took a swing at him."

Fleshman said, "But you didn't hit him. Is that right?

Finnell just nodded.

Then Fleshman said, "You left the Dean's office about eight? Did you see anyone else in the building?"

"No, but I was furious and I wasn't looking for anyone." He shrugged and added, "Someone could have been there, I suppose."

"And the Dean was alive when you left his office?

"Yes, he certainly was."

"You walked across campus to the basketball game, got there about 8:15, and stayed there until the game was over.

"That's right."

Fleshman looked him for a long moment. Then he said, "You know I can book you for breaking and entering. And threatening Dr. Crashaw with a gun."

Fleshman's voice was sharp.

For a moment I let myself enjoy the sight of Finnell squirming, and a picture of him in jail with a bunch of degenerates and drunks floated joyously into my mind.

All I had to do was press charges.

But eventually he would get out and be back at the University, and he would be a deadly enemy. It wasn't worth it.

So I said, "I don't want to press charges. Let it go."

Fleshman looked both surprised and chagrined. He said, "Are you sure?"

I nodded.

He said to Finnell, "I'll keep the gun until you bring your permit to the station. You can go, but don't leave town again."

As soon as he was out the door, I hurried to let Tess out of the closet. She crept out slowly, eyed me, and meowed plaintively, her way of telling me that I had been derelict in her care.

I picked her up and checked her over to see if Finnell had hurt her. She understood my concern and lay quietly while I probed. She seemed all right, nothing was broken.

Apparently Finnell had simply pushed her out of his way. I was glad. I would have planned something harmful for him if he had hurt her.

I handed Jake a cup of coffee, and said, "I'm happy the nightmare with Finnell is over. He scared me out of my mind, but I don't think he murdered anybody."

"Why not?"

"Because he's a gutless coward."

"Doesn't take courage to kill, just passion."

"He finally told the truth about being there, didn't he? That's why he was so scared. Why he ran."

Jake's eyes were thoughtful. "He may be smarter than you think. It's an old trick, to divert suspicion from one thing by confessing to something else."

"Then he's not off your suspect list?" I thought about Aunt Grace's firm conclusion that Finnell wasn't the murderer.

"No one is until I get either a confession or irrefutable evidence that will solve the murders."

"Can I help?"

He laughed. "You're still interested? After being, as you said, scared out of your mind?"

"Try me."

"Okay. I want to check Herndon's and Parson's alibi that they were at the Blue Boar the night that Dean Stafford was killed. It sounds suspicious, but maybe the people who work there will be able to verify or deny it."

He smiled and said, "I would like it very much if you could meet me there about nine o'clock tomorrow night?"

I said, "Of course I can."

"Good," he said.

I was pleased that he would ask me to go along with him. Maybe he thought I had handled myself well with Finnell.

I walked him to the door. He stopped and said "Tomorrow get a dead bolt put on your French doors. Finnell got inside your house using a credit card."

Chapter 24

My relief that the Finnell episode had turned out reasonably well boosted my morale. To my way of thinking, he was no longer a viable suspect of the murder of the Dean or Clarence even though Fleshman had reservations about his innocence.

Finnell's four day absence from the university and his encounter with Detective Fleshman had served to humble him a bit, and I had hope that he wouldn't be quite so difficult to deal with, at least for a few weeks or so.

On Monday morning I walked down the hall to his classroom. He was standing just outside the door and his "Good morning, Dr. Crashaw" was both polite and respectful, untainted by his usual corrosively satirical and demeaning tone.

I replied, "Good morning, Dr. Finnell. We're glad you're back from your fishing trip." That last statement, of course, was for the benefit of the students who milled around in the hallway, probably curious to know where he had been the past few days.

He could elaborate on my statement to explain his absence. I imagined he would either use the tired excuse of car trouble or concoct some horrendous tale of getting lost on the lake and barely making his way back to the shore. Or he might come up with something more ingenious that would help him save face.

I marched past the group toward my office, feeling safer than I had in days because at least I knew that Finnell had been the prowler, not some crazy pervert out to do me in. I wanted to believe, I guess, along with Robert Browning, that for the time being anyway, "God's in his heaven, and all's right with the world." I should have known better.

God may be in his heaven, but in the academic arena seldom is everything all right with the students or their world.

As if to bring my attention back to the problems of that academic world, I found two students waiting outside my office.

One was James Morris, a second year teaching assistant and the other was an attractive woman whom I recognized as a graduate student. I couldn't remember her name.

I smiled at them and said, "I'll see you in a minute. Which one of you is first?"

The woman motioned toward James, but he said, "She can go first. I got your note to check by your office, but I've got a class in five minutes. I'll be back after it is over."

I wondered if he would. Until recently, he had been one of our brightest and best teachers, but something had happened, and several complaints had been lodged against him. Thus the need for a conference.

I hadn't a clue as to what the woman's problem might be. I motioned her into the office to sit down. While I unloaded my briefcase, I watched her. She was well-groomed and attractive with dark hair and clear blue eyes. She looked to be in her early thirties. Except for her hands, which were clasped tightly in her lap, she seemed poised and at ease.

I smiled and said, "You're one of our graduate students, I know, but I've forgotten your name."

"I'm Diane Barrett," she said. "I will graduate in the spring."

A bell went off in my head. She was the student who was bringing a sexual harassment suit against Dr. Parsons. I remembered that she had taken a course in Milton from me. She had been an excellent student.

I said, "I remember you now, Diane. What can I help you with?"

She was watching me carefully and said, "I'm bringing a sexual harassment suit against Dr. Parsons."

Why come to me now? I thought. I had been left out of the loop because Diane had skipped my office and gone directly to Dean Stafford with her complaint, apparently not wanting to talk to me as Chairperson.

But now, of course, the Dean was dead, and could not support her claim.

I didn't really feel too concerned about her and her problem, so I said, "I see," keeping my voice as non-committal as I could. I had no desire to get involved in a harassment petition that could easily end up in a messy court trial. I wanted no part of suits, or lawyers, or anything remotely connected with the judicial system.

She was waiting for me to add something to my ubiquitous "I see." I obliged her by asking the question again, "How can I help you?"

"I'm going to continue the suit even without Dean Stafford's help."

"I see." I repeated. I was thinking, *How can I avoid getting involved?* The answer floated up from somewhere in my unconscious mind. *Keep the problem squarely in the new Dean's office.*

I said, "You need to take your problem to Dean Hawkins. He will be glad to hear your accusations and perhaps be able to take actions that will be adequate for you."

"I want to give you the details," she said, defiance in her voice. I didn't need for her to recite the details.

This scenario had been played out by Parsons too many times. She had been a student in his class, he had put a move on her, she had been flattered, they had ended up in bed. Then he had tired of her and now she was a woman scorned and determined to get even. I wasn't having any part of it.

"Since you originally registered your complaint with the Dean's office, that's where you should go, Mrs. Barrett. I'm sure Dean Hawkins will be able to help you."

Her eyes were angry, and her lips had thinned. "Then you won't listen to what I have to say?"

I was tired of both her complaint and her attitude. I stood up. "You lodged your complaint with the Dean. I'm not going to be presumptuous and try to take anything out of his hands."

Her face reddened. "Then I'll tell him that you refused to listen to a legitimate complaint and that you are covering for one of your professors."

I felt my own face flush. I said, "You do whatever you want, but right now you'll have to excuse me. I have work to do."

She gave me a long silent stare, but finally turned and walked out. I closed the door behind her, muttering "Damn Parsons and his overactive libido."

I knew we hadn't heard the last from her. I was also convinced she was not a naive young thing who had been seduced by Parsons.

She was an adult and I assumed she had entered into a sexual relationship with her eyes wide open. And the last time I checked, consensual sex between adults was not a crime.

The only problem I could visualize was if she had a smart lawyer he might find a loophole and determine that Parsons could be charged with lewd conduct unbecoming a professor.

I sensed a steely determination in her that didn't bode well for Parsons, but that was his problem, not mine. I quickly put the incident out of my mind.

I was more concerned about my scheduled meeting with James Morris, our teaching assistant. What was bothering him? Why would he suddenly be having all kinds of trouble with his students? Why would he mess up his chances of being hired as a full-time professor?

I waited until four-thirty, hoping he would come by and talk with me as he had promised. But he didn't show up, which meant I would have to re-schedule a meeting with him.

Tired and anxious to leave, I was busy cramming papers and books into my brief case when the phone rang. It was Fleshman. He said, "Don't forget that I'm picking you up about nine o'clock. For our trip to the Blue Boar. "

"I'll be ready," I said.

"I will be double checking the alibis of Herndon and Parsons."

"I know," I said. "Good idea,"

I hung up the phone. I sat staring at the desk for several minutes, thinking of how thorough Fleshman was in dealing with suspects. Then the recent scene with Diane Barrett came back to bother me. I knew in my gut that Parsons was guilty of having sex with her, and now she was on a rampage to get even.

No doubt it would be a messy situation before it was solved. But despite the sordidness of Parsons affairs and the continuing drinking problem of Herndon, I wasn't too concerned that either of them had anything to do about Stafford's death.

Their alibis had been fairly straight forward. They were drinking themselves stupid at the Blue Boar during the time that someone had killed the Dean.

I glanced outside my office window. The sky had cleared and a beautiful orange-red Oklahoma sunset flamed across the sky.

It looked like the severe winter storms that had buried us in snow and ice for the past several weeks had finally broken. A few sunny days would melt the snow and ice into slush.

I thought of Matt's plan for us to fly to San Diego, and it sounded more and more appealing. To loll in the sun for a few days would do both my body and my soul good, and to get away from the anxiety and stress of the past days was even more alluring.

I roused myself from my day dreaming, remembered I had a date to meet Fleshman for the Blue Boar excursion, and quickly began gathering material to stuff in my brief case.

I took a long look around the room to be sure I wasn't leaving anything, turned toward the doorway, ready to flip out the lights.

There stood Eddie Parsons, lounging against the doorway. "We need to talk," he said, walking past me to slouch down in a chair across from my desk.

I didn't want to deal with him. I said tartly, "I'm leaving for the day."

"This won't take long," he said, pulling himself up and sitting on the edge of his chair. "I heard that Diane Barrett was in to see you. What did she have to say?

I stopped in my tracks and wondered *How had he learned that she had been here?*

I resented his insolent assumption that I would tell him all about the meeting. "She mentioned the harassment suit she's filing against you."

"Did she ask you to testify against me?"

"I told her that the Dean was in charge of the problem."

He said, "You didn't answer my question. Will you take Barrett's side? You know that whatever happened between her and me was because she wanted it."

His smile was sly. "I don't have to beg for it, you know."

I took a deep breath and said, "I don't care about your personal sex life, Dr. Parsons, and I have no intention of being drawn into your personal predicament."

I paused a second, and added, "And make no mistake, you *do have* a problem. Barrett isn't some silly freshman you can seduce and then toss aside. She is very upset, and she is out to get you if she can. Personally, I think she's going to give you more grief than you ever imagined."

"You sound happy at the prospect."

I felt my face flushing with anger. I wanted to tell him how happy I was that someone his age had taken him on. I had dealt with too many sobbing undergraduates who had refused to lodge a complaint against him.

I moved around my desk toward the door and opened it. "You can go now. This conversation is over."

Slowly, he stood up. His eyes were blue ice and he moved toward me until he was almost in my face.

Then he said, "Dean Stafford made a big mistake when he decided he'd support Barrett instead of me. He ended up dead."

I didn't flinch. "You go to hell, Parsons."

"Watch your back, Dr. Crashaw," he said as he pushed by me and out the door.

Chapter 25

All the way home I thought about Eddie Parsons and his parting threat. "Watch your back," he had said. Maybe it was an idle threat made in the heat of the moment and didn't mean anything. Or maybe it did.

One thing I knew for sure. I was on his hate list because I wouldn't defend him against Barrett.

I went into the house and threw my briefcase down in a chair. I was so tired that when I dropped on the bed. I was almost instantly asleep.

It was almost nine o'clock when the doorbell's ringing awakened me. I jumped up and headed to the door with Tess marching along with me. She waited as I checked the peephole before I opened the door.

Jake, grinned. "I guess Tess is beginning to recognize me. Are you ready to go?"

"We're still checking out the Blue Boar tonight?"

"That's it."

"Can you wait five minutes while I freshen up. I have been asleep.

"No problem," he said.

It took me more than five minutes, but he just smiled when I came back in, and said, "You look good."

We walked to the black and white patrol car he was driving, and he helped me in.

I felt a little conspicuous. I had always looked with suspicion at a woman who was riding in a police car, assuming that she was either a desperate criminal or an unsavory pick-up.

He guided the car cautiously through the slush that was beginning to freeze into a thin layer of ice. The warming trend had only lasted until the sun went down, and the temperature was dropping. He glanced at me and asked, "How was your day?"

"I've had better," I said, managing a laugh. "I practically threw Dr. Parsons out of my office."

"Remember you told me about those papers you found at the Dean's house? The ones about Parsons being charged with sexual harassment? Well, the student bringing the charges, who incidentally is a mature woman, was in my office today."

"Parsons had found out about it and came in to warn me about the danger of defending her. He said, "Stafford made that mistake and ended up dead."

"That was when I told him to get out."

"Do you think he is dangerous, that he might hurt you?"

I thought a moment, then said, "Not really. He's a predator with women, but he hasn't the courage necessary to hurt anyone. At least that's how I would evaluate him."

"Do you think he's guilty of harassment?"

"Probably not in this case. The woman is thirtyish and divorced. I think it's more likely a case of a woman scorned after a torrid affair and wanting to get even. 'Hell hath no fury,' the poet said."

"What is it about teaching English that makes men nuts? All your professors seem to have major problems with their libido."

"Not *just* the men." I said, thinking of Helen Stafford.

He grinned. "I don't think I'll comment on that."

I felt my face getting hot, and I changed the subject.

"Why are you checking out Parsons and Herndon again? Anything new about their alibis?"

"No. It's just that their story that they were drinking themselves into a stupor the night the Dean was killed is a little too convenient. It troubles me. From what you've told me, Herndon is an alcoholic and I can see him getting stone drunk, but what about Parsons? Is he a regular drinker? And do they often get drunk together? Particularly on Sunday nights?

I didn't bother to answer his questions. I don't think he expected me to. I said, "It's hard to guess why they might be doing anything at any particular time."

When we pulled up into the Blue Boar parking lot, I glanced across the street at the University campus. Usually cars overflowed from the Blue Boar on to the campus parking lot, but tonight there were only a few cars huddled outside.

A clumsy looking pig outlined by blue neon lights perched on top of the L shaped building and blinked the message that this was indeed the Blue Boar.

We got out of the car and walked to the garishly painted pink front door. We walked in.

The large room was comfortably warm but the heavy smell of innumerable beers mixed unpleasantly with the odor of grilled onions and seared hamburger meat.

Surprisingly there was not the layer of blue cigarette smoke usually found in most bars. I found out later that the owner had emphysema and rigidly enforced a no smoking rule.

It took a moment for my eyes to adjust to the dim lighting. Several tables were spaced haphazardly about the room, and I saw three college young men lounging at one of them. I didn't recognize anyone, but apparently one of them knew me. He raised his hand and waved. I waved back.

Fleshman walked to the bar where the bartender, a youngish man in a red turtleneck, was vigorously wiping the oaken top with a towel.

He looked up at him and said, "What's your pleasure, Detective?"

Fleshman said, "I was in here a couple of weeks ago and talked to you about two professors from the University being here on a particular Sunday night. Remember?"

He grinned. "Yeah. They really tied one on that night."

"Where did they do their drinking?"

"They had a booth at the back."

He slapped the towel down and came around the bar.

"I'll show you."

We followed him around the L to a corner booth, one of four in that area.

He pointed. "That's their booth. They ordered three drinks each and lined them up. They were here for serious drinking."

"How long did they stay?"

He scratched his head. "They came in, oh, around eight o'clock, just before the crowd began to get heavy. I don't know when they left. One of them came and ordered another round just before nine o'clock."

Fleshman said, "The time they stayed here is important. They swore they were here from eight until about ten thirty."

He shrugged his shoulders, "I don't know. Could've been. We were busy and I wasn't paying attention."

"Did anybody else see them?"

"I don't know. Like I said, we were all busy that night."

"So you can't say for sure that they were here all the time?"

"Nope. Sorry."

Fleshman turned to me and said, "Do you want something to eat? drink?"

"Coffee would be good."

"Bring us two coffees."

He motioned me toward the booth and we sat down. I could hear the juke box beating out a country western song, the rattle of beer bottles, and an occasional laugh.

`"Nice booth, " I said. "Quiet and private."

"A good place to do some serious drinking, if you're so inclined. And from what I hear, your profs were often so inclined."

I said, "I don't think Herndon is ever completely sober. So far he's been able to handle his classes, but one of these days he is going to fall out. The coffee cup he carries to class is filled with peppermint vodka."

"He's not very smart, is he? If he's a boozer. What about Parsons?"

"He is a binge drinker. He will go for months without a drink and then get roaring drunk."

The red shirted bar tender brought back two coffees and a full carafe. "So you won't be bothered," he said.

His smile was sly, and I had the feeling that these back booths were used for more than just serious drinking.

I took a sip of coffee and said, "What are you looking for here, Jake?"

He sat across from me, facing the back of the room. "I don't know. I just like to double check alibis. Sometimes something develops." His voice trailed off.

He was staring over my shoulder. Suddenly he got up, went to the back door and slipped outside, letting a draft of cold air sweep in.

In a minute or two, he was back inside. Amused at his fidgety behavior I said, "What's going on?

He said, "I need to borrow your keys to the LA Building for just a spell. "I want to try something."

He looked so serious that I started digging in my purse for the keys and handed them to him. I smiled and said, "Want to tell me what you're up to?"

"Do something for me. Sit right here, check your watch and tell me exactly how many minutes before I get back."

He was out the door again. I looked around, but the other booths were empty.

I felt a little foolish sitting there by myself, but I glanced at my watch to check the time. I was about to go to the bar for a fresh carafe of coffee when the door opened and Jake hurried inside, shaking the snow off his coat.

"How long?" he asked, "exactly how long?"

I looked at my watch. "Exactly twenty-six minutes. But it seemed like an hour."

He snapped his fingers and looked at me, a satisfied look on his face. "It could be done."

"What you are talking about?"

"Did the bartender come back while I was gone?"

"No, but what. . . ?"

"He hasn't been here since we first came in, over an hour ago, has he?"

I was about to lose patience. He was doing an Aunt Grace number on me -- ignoring my questions and making no sense. What difference did it make whether the bartender checked on us or not?

"No, he has not" I said, "but what's that got to do with anything?"

"Okay, listen to me. I walked across campus to the LA Building, opened the door, walked directly to the Dean's office, stood there for ten minutes, then turned around and got back here in twenty-six minutes. I could probably have been gone another twenty minutes and still have returrned before anyone in the bar knew I was not here."

"All right. So what?"

"It proves that either Herndon or Parsons could have slipped out this back door, killed the Dean, and returned without anyone knowing he was gone."

"But that's too bizarre for anything. You don't just jump up, leave your drinking buddy, and dash off to kill someone.

And even if you wanted to, how could you slip out without your friend knowing it?"

"Easy. If your buddy is so drunk he has passed out. It could be done."

I was beginning to understand what he was getting at. "So you think that Herndon passed out and Parsons saw his chance to kill the Dean?"

"I think it is possible. You told me Herndon is the heavy drinker, and Parsons knew that. He could have engineered the whole thing and set himself up with a near perfect alibi."

I remembered Parson's icy eyes and his parting threat, and I was uncomfortably aware that Fleshman might be right.

I said, "What are you going to do?"

His eyes were thoughtful.

"I'm going to question him again. Put the pressure on, make him very nervous if I can. Maybe he will do something foolish."

"Like what?"

"I don't know. Maybe he will get scared and say something incriminating, either about himself or Herndon."

I said, "Maybe I can help."

Immediately his face darkened. "No. I don't want you to do anything, Connie. I just wanted to bounce these ideas off you to see what you think. I'll take care of putting the case together and finding the murderer."

I said, "I know you will. But I'm around Herndon and Parsons every day. I can watch them, maybe even toss out a few innuendos. . . ."

"No. It would be too dangerous."

"I would be very careful."

"Absolutely not."

I decided not to push. "Okay," I said.

I looked at him appraisingly. What would he say if he knew of my plan to put the pressure on Munsell to get a promotion? I wasn't about to tell him and find out. That was my own personal and private agenda.

Chapter **26**

I still had to deal with the problem of Jimmy Morris, our student teacher. When I got to my office the next day, I sent Rosa with a note to his classroom, asking him to come to my office immediately after the class was over.

When I had hired him, I had thought he would be a good candidate for a permanent teaching position, and I was not going to let him mess up his career without at least finding out what his problem was.

Right now he was doing all the wrong things. Two girls had come by to report that his lectures were not making sense. They hinted that maybe drugs were involved.

Another young man had reported last week that Jimmy had stopped his lecture, closed his book, and without any explanation left the room and had not returned.

I needed to give him a chance to explain, and I was fearful that he might not come by my office. He had not come by the first time I had asked him. But this time he did. He appeared in my doorway right on time.

As always, I was impressed with his dark good looks and his careful grooming, but there was a difference in him from the cheerful and grateful young man I had hired to teach. His smile, usually warm and happy, was gone, and he wouldn't look at me directly, but kept glancing nervously around the room.

I said, "Thanks for coming by."

I hoped he would feel comfortable and maybe bring up whatever was bothering him.

"Yeah," he said, cautiously lowering himself into the chair across from me. His eyes were focused on the small window to the left of my desk.

"How are things going? With your classes, I mean?"

His answer was short and abrupt, a noncommittal "Okay."

He seemed determined to answer in monosyllables and to avoid looking at me.

I decided to get to the point. "Are you having trouble with any of your students?"

"Not that I know of." His voice was slightly belligerent, and he was rubbing the sides of his jeans as if they were binding his legs.

I was puzzled. He was completely out of character, nothing like the polite, conscientious young student I had hired.

"Well," I said, "That's odd. Several students have complained about the way you have been conducting your class."

"Is that so? Well, tough for them."

His defiance was so completely unexpected that I reacted in turn. "Do you want to know what they have complained about?"

He said, "No. I don't care."

"You should," I said. "And unless you've got a good reason for what's been happening, you are in trouble."

His face reddened and his eyes flashed. "You're threatening to fire me?"

"Give me a reason not to, an explanation . . . ."

The muscles in his jaw were working overtime, and his lips had thinned. I could feel the pent up anger and frustration radiating from him.

I waited a moment longer, hoping he would get control and open up with me. Finally, I said, "What's bothering you? Talk to me, Jimmy."

His face suddenly crumpled and tears brightened his eyes. "You won't have to fire me, I'm leaving anyway." His hopeless tone upset me more than his insolence had.

I tried again "What's happening, Jimmy? Maybe I can help."

His head dropped and his voice was very low. "I already

talked to Dean Stafford." His voice trailed off.

"You talked to Dean Stafford? When? Why?"

"A week before he was killed. He said he would do something."

"Do something about what?"

He swallowed convulsively a couple of times and then he said, "The Dean promised me he would call Dr. Finnell into his office and talk to him. "

I was surprised, and I didn't really know what to say for a moment. Then I said, "Okay, what did you tell the Dean about Dr.Finnell? I knew that Jimmy was taking one of Finnell's classes and my first thought was that he had probably given him a bad grade..

He said, "I told the Dean about something that happened at the Christmas party."

I said, "Okay, I know about that party, now tell me what happened."

He glanced quickly at me and then dropped his eyes as if looking at me was upsetting him. He said, "I talked to the Dean about it. Do I have to talk to you?"

I was becoming impatient. "Yes, you do, Jimmy. You do remember that Dean Stafford is dead? So you need to tell me what this is all about."

His voice when he spoke was that of an automaton.

"Well, Dr. Finnell. . . ." He stopped again.

I said, as firmly as I could, "Jimmy, no more stalling. Get on with it!"

I guess my tone scared him.

He began to speak as rapidly as he could. "I told the Dean what Dr. Finnell said to me. After the party, he came over and he asked me to stay and help him clean up, and I said I would. And while I was picking up stuff and everything, he came over and put his arm around me and he . . . touched me and then he tried to persuade me to . . . do what he wanted, and when I said no, he got real angry and promised to ruin me at the University."

I knew my face reflected the shock I was feeling. I had not been prepared for this.

He said, "I never had a chance to see Dean Stafford again. He got himself killed before he could do anything.

My head was spinning. Finnell had admitted being in the Dean's office early that evening but he had said it was because he was defending himself against a black woman's accusation.

But the Dean had addressed him about something much more serious. The charge of trying to molest a student was a sure way to be fired, whether one had tenure or not.

I could imagine what happened. The Dean, glad to have something on Finnell, had confronted him, and probably threatened to fire him. Finnell, acting in character, had probably lost control and in a blind, unreasoning rage struck him, not with his fist as he had said, but with a lethal statue and killed him!

I was stunned. My mind was spinning and I didn't know what to say to Jimmy. The best if could manage was, "And this is why you've been so upset in class?"

"Yes," he said, his face miserable. "So you don't have to worry about firing me. I'll get through this semester and leave as quickly as I can. I don't ever want to teach at a university again."

A sense of sadness swept over me. He was a young, idealistic student who had experienced the dark side of someone he trusted. It would be useless to try to dissuade him from leaving or convince him that there was any reason for him to stay in the teaching profession. The heart had gone out of him.

My response was feeble and wholly inadequate. I said, "I'm sorry, Jimmy, truly sorry. If I can help… " My voice trailed off.

He managed a tenuous smile and said, "I'll be okay," and left .I watched him go and cursed my helplessness to make things right for him. I was depressed and angry.

I grabbed the phone and dialed Fleshman's office. I wanted to tell him that Finnell had lied about *why* he had been in the Dean's office that night, and that I really thought he could easily have erupted into a killing rage.

Fleshman didn't answer the phone, but I knew he would return my call immediately.

I tried to put all that had happened out of my mind so I could calm down and be able to do some kind of work. I needed to make a test for my class in Shakespeare, so I concentrated on that particular task. I worked steadily and by the time I had structured four discussion questions, it was four thirty. I sighed, looked over the exam questions one more time for any errors.

The exam looked good. I stretched my back and decided I'd go home early. As I pushed back my chair, the phone rang.

I grabbed it, thinking it was Fleshman.

To my surprise, it was Vice President Munsell. His voice was friendly and solicitous, which sent off alarm bells in my brain.

"I'm glad I caught you, Dr. Crashaw; I've been intending to call for several days. How are things in the English department?"

Going to hell in a hand basket, but what's that to you, you creep?

"Busy." I said. "Complicated as every new semester is."

I still had no idea why he was calling. It certainly wasn't to find out how things were with me.

He said, "I understand completely. So much of what we do in academia is complicated and difficult."

I waited. Something was up with him.

He managed a huge sigh, and then said, "I want you to know that choosing the new dean for Liberal Arts was one of those more difficult decisions."

He waited for a response, but I remained quiet. If he had something else to say, he would have to say it without any encouragement from me.

Finally he said, "I also want you to know that you were one of the top two applicants, Dr. Crashaw."

"Oh, really?" I did not even try to keep the heavy sarcasm out of my voice.

He cleared his throat and replied "Yes, you were right up there with Dr. Hawkins. It was, as I said, a terribly difficult choice. But Dr. Hawkins had seniority and that finally was the deciding factor."

Another pause. "We have to honor longevity, you know." His voice had now become conciliatory, even cloying.

I found myself choking back rage. The confusion and anguish about the death of Stafford and Clarence, the disillusionment and loss of a student like Jimmy, the whole stinking mess that was the academic world merged in my mind with a chaotic fury that shook my very bones.

My voice trembled but I said, "I understand perfectly. I understand that you have to take all kinds of facts under consideration when you make your very important and fateful decisions. And, I'm sure you were very conscientious in making your choice to promote Hawkins to Dean."

He sounded surprised, but happy about my reaction. He said, "I'm glad you understand."

Struggling to control my anger, I said, "And I'm confident you will be equally conscientious when this year's requests for promotion to full professor reach your office."

"Of course."

"And I will very grateful and pleased to learn that I am being promoted to full professor."

His voice became careful, guarded. He said, "Well, er, yes, your promotion is certainly a possibility."

I spoke slowly and carefully. I said, "No, a *possibility* is not acceptable, Dr. Munsell. I *will be* the one you promote to full professor."

"Well, I can hardly promise that . . . "

"Oh, yes, I think you can. And I am sure that you will."

I paused again, hearing him drawing in his breath, knowing that my arrogance was kindling his anger.

I savored the moment for a nanosecond before I said, "I found the Stafford file you have been inquiring about."

I waited, giving him time to absorb the lie and the implications of it. It was an unmitigated lie, of course, but I was in such a mental state that the lie slid off my tongue as easily as any truth ever had. What followed was a very heavy silence.

Then he said, "I see. You have the file in your possession right now." He paused a second, and then added, "And you read the file?"

"Of course I did."

His voice had become poisonous. He flared, "You had no business reading it."

"But I did. And I intend to use it to get my promotion, you bastard."

I could imagine his fury because he knew that I had won.

Finally, he got control of himself and said, "When can I get this file?"

"I will bring it to you *after* I have received the official confirmation from the President's office that I have been promoted to full professor."

Another long silence followed. Then he said, 'Did you make a copy of it?"

I said, "No, I did not. And I will not. I have the original copy only and I will not make any copies to hold over your head. I will give the file to you when our agreement is fulfilled."

He seemed calmer when he said, "I think I understand. Quid pro quo, Dr. Crashaw?"

"Quid pro quo, Dr. Munsell."

Another long pause. Then a click, and the line went dead.

I felt a kind of frenzied exultation. I had done it. I had thrown down the gauntlet, and he had been forced to pick it up. I was elated, but even then I think at some unconscious level I realized that what I had done was dangerous and that I was on a slippery slope. But it didn't matter.

I had beat Munsell at his own game. That was good enough for me.

Chapter 27

I don't remember driving through the late afternoon traffic home. Usually the hectic flow of cars darting in and out of lanes and the occasional angry motorist hitting his horn in protest to an imagined wrong made me both nervous and very cautious.

Not today. I swung from lane to lane with the best of them, hitting my horn when I felt like it. I was on an emotional high. The adrenalin was flowing, and I was proud of myself.

I had out-foxed and out manipulated an unscrupulous and political vice president into giving me the promotion I absolutely deserved, and I felt completely justified in what I had done.

He had promoted a weak and incompetent crony to the position of dean, and I hadn't been able to do anything about that, but I had been able to do something for myself so that I would receive a full professorship this year.

I had no plan as to how I would handle Munsell when he found out that I had been lying about the Stafford file. It hadn't seemed important at the moment, and I was not going to worry about it now.

I pulled into the driveway and hurried into the front door. Since Finnell had broken in by slipping a credit card in the door, I had changed all the locks for heavier ones.

Once inside, I called for Tess. Her appearance in the hallway reassured me that all was well. She marched alongside me as I went into the bedroom to change clothes.

Matt had once said that Tess heeled like a well-trained dog, but I knew it was her way of affirming that she was with me, that we were partners.

"I stuck up for myself today, Tess" I said. "No more waiting for someone in Administration to recognize that I'm deserving of promotion. I took action to make sure that I get a full professorship this year."

She had leapt into the recliner chair near the bed. She flattened out and nuzzled her head against the arm rest. Her black eyes followed me as I changed into jeans and a T-shirt. "It means you get fresh salmon instead of canned tuna, and I can afford T-bone steaks for a change." I reached down and stroked her gently on her back. She raised her head and rubbed against my hand. "It means that I'm taking control of what happens to me, Tess, and to hell with everyone else."

Suddenly the doorbell rang. Tess jumped off the chair and followed me down the hallway. I had to smile at her sticking so close beside me. "Don't worry. I won't open the door unless it's a friend."

It was Aunt Grace. When Tess saw who it was, she turned and ran. I think Aunt Grace gives off some kind of scent that warns Tess that she doesn't like her. Aunt Grace sailed inside, pulling her coat aside, and heading for the kitchen. "I need a cup of tea, Constance," she huffed. "I've just had an extraordinary experience."

"A good one or a bad one?" I asked as I followed her. I put the tea kettle on the burner while I rummaged for a tea bag.

"I'm not absolutely sure," she said as she sat down. "That's why I wanted to talk to you."

I finally found a box with three orange pekoe bags. "It'll have to be plain tea, Aunt Grace, but I've got some coffee creamer that will jazz it up for you."

"Whatever. Just be sure it's boiling hot."

I waited until the tea kettle whistled before I poured the water over the tea bag. I handed it to her and said, "Now tell me about this extraordinary experience."

She took a quick sip of the scalding tea and said, "Do you have lemon, Constance?"

I sighed. She had completely ignored what I had said about the coffee creamer. I got up and searched the fridge. I had long ago learned that you don't rush Aunt Grace into anything. She moves at her own pace or not at all. I found a lemon, sliced it, and handed the slice to her. She promptly dropped it into the teacup, swirled it around with her spoon, and took another sip.

"Ah, that's good," she said. Suddenly she looked around the room. "Where is that cat?" Her voice sounded as if she were asking about a coiled cobra ready to strike.

"Tess retreated to my bedroom as soon as she saw you. Now tell me what happened."

She took a sip of tea. "Well, you know how much I enjoy lunch at the Victorian House. I was there to meet my friend Pearl, but she phoned and said she couldn't make it. An upset stomach, or something. Anyway, I just settled in by myself to enjoy their special of the day, a chicken-filled tomato."

So far I hadn't heard anything exciting or unusual. I was pretty sure she wasn't excited about the stuffed tomato, so I waited patiently.

Aunt Grace's eyes widened over the edge of her tea cup. "That's when I saw this man. Looking at me. Actually he was staring at me."

"That's understandable. You're a good looking woman."

Her eyebrows shot up. "Don't be facetious, Constance."

"I'm not. You *are* handsome." I was having trouble keeping a straight face. The picture of her fending off a man struck me as hilarious.

I said, "The important thing is, was *he* good-looking?"

Her back straightened. She carefully placed her cup down in front of her. "I won't say another word. You are not being serious about this."

I felt properly chastened. I reached out and patted her hand. "I'm sorry. Go ahead."

She gave me a long look. "Well, finally he got up, came over to my table, introduced himself as Max Ernhart, and asked me if I had been a student at Hardin-Simmons University in the fifties." She paused, waiting for my reaction.

"And you said?"

"That I had attended the University of Texas. And he said I looked very much like someone he knew in college. Again she paused. "He was very polite, and he stood there looking embarrassed." She took a deep breath. "I invited him to sit down."

"Okay," I said, drawing out the word. "And then?"

Her eyes lighted up. "We had a nice visit. He is a retired colonel in the Air Force, and he has been all over the world. He's widowed and has two grown boys. And he wants to see me again."

"What did you say?"

"I said he could call me next week. I liked him,"

I wasn't quite sure how to respond. I didn't want to make the mistake of trying to tell her what to do, or what not to do, but I was apprehensive. He could be a slick con man up to no good.

She seemed to have read my mind. She said, "Don't worry. In a week, Detective Fleshman will have him checked out. I'll know all I need to know about him."

I stuttered, "You mean you've talked to Fleshman about this? Asked him to check this man out?"

It was her turn to look surprised. "Of course. The Detective and I are friends. He'll call me in a day or so."

I shook my head in amazement. "Aunt Grace, I can't believe . . . ." I was saved from making a real gaffe by the ringing of the telephone.

It was Fleshman. He began, "That offer you made to help. Did you mean it?"

"Of course."

"I've got two tickets to the opera at Tulsa tomorrow night, and I need someone to go with me. Are you available?"

I was caught completely off balance. How could going to the opera have anything to do with catching a murderer?

I said, "You think the murderer is an opera fan?"

He laughed. "No, I am the opera fan. But I want to check an alibi, and I thought you might enjoy the sleuthing along with the opera."

"Who's got a Tulsa alibi?"

"Your friend Matt. Remember? He was working in Tulsa the night Stafford was murdered."

I was so surprised that for a moment I didn't know what to say. "But you don't think . . ?"

"I double check everybody. Remember? Sometimes it is the second time around that something develops. Or I get a new idea. The question is, would you like to join me?"

I hesitated a moment. I liked the idea of going to the opera. I liked the idea of sleuthing along with Fleshman to find the murderer, but I wondered a bit at his decision to check Matt's alibi.

And then I thought *"I'll bet he has checked me out!"* and then I felt a little foolish.

Of course, he had checked me out. Hadn't he told Matt and me just recently that he checked out every suspect more than once?

I laughed at my own seriousness and said, "I'd love to go, but you're wasting your time checking Matt."

He said, "The opera is <u>Aida</u>. You'll love it. I'll pick you up at five." He hung up.

I looked at Aunt Grace and said, "That was your comrade, Detective Fleshman."

A satisfied smile spread over her face. "He's a very nice man."

I had to agree.

Chapter 28

The sun was a flaming ball descending on the horizon as Jake and I headed east on the turnpike to Tulsa and the opera. The sun had been strong all day, but the road was still wet in spots. Banks of snow had begun to melt, and rivulets of water flooded the fields alongside the road.

I sat back and relaxed in Jake's five-year-old black Volvo as it purred down the road. I didn't say anything for several minutes then I turned toward him and said, "I've something to tell you about Finnell that may put him at the top of your suspect list again."

"Oh," he said, "What's that?"

I told him Jimmy Morris' story. I explained that according to Jimmy's account, the real reason Stafford had called Finnell on the carpet that Sunday night was to tell him he was going to take disciplinary action against him.

When I told him that Finnell had tried to hit Stafford, his interest quickened. He asked, "How do you think Finnell reacted to the Dean's threat to call the Campus police?"

"He would have been furious."

"Would Finnell be capable of violence?"

I thought about his question for a long minute. I didn't want to make a mistake about Finnell, but I thought of his paranoia and his quick temper and I said, "Yes."

"Then I'll bring him in for questioning again."

I said, "He will deny everything, of course, and say that Jimmy lied about the whole thing."

I paused. "How do you ever sort it all out? Find out the truth about anything? Especially about a murder?"

He thought a minute before he answered. "You keep working, following leads, checking and re-checking. And you hope for a break."

"Do you always find the murderer?"

"No, not always. We have cases that have never been solved. But I think I will solve this one."

"Why?"

"Because I think the murderer is someone connected with the University, and he, or she, can't leave, can't get away from the scene of the crime. And eventually he will make a mistake."

I glanced at him. He looked elegant in his tux, more like an orchestra leader than a homicide detective.

I said, "It surprised me to find out that you're an opera buff."

He grinned. "It's all because of my Aunt Velma. When I was a teenager I used to visit her during the summer. She taught music in the Santa Fe High School and wanted me, her favorite nephew, to appreciate more than just the Beatles.

"So, we made a deal. She'd buy me the newest rock'n'roll album if I'd go to the opera with her. I thought it was a good trade-off, and I ended up getting hooked on Verdi and others of his kind."

I said, "Speaking of aunts, I understand that Aunt Grace has been asking favors of you again."

"She needed to find out about a man who is apparently interested in her." He cut his eyes toward me and smiled. "She's a sharp lady, and I like her style."

"And?"

"And what?"

"What did you find out about this man?"

"He's a serial killer from Boston who preys on old ladies and female college professors."

"Jake!"

His eyes were twinkling. "Okay. Okay. He's a reputable bank robber. His last job was a Brinks armored car, and he got away with a million or so."

"You're pretty funny, Detective Fleshman. Probably should try for a gig at Jokers Club. They need fresh talent."

"He is just what he said he was, a retired military man. Last duty was in Massachusetts, just before he came here. He's pretty well connected. He has friends with one or two college presidents in Massachusetts. He was a visiting lecturer at Amherst and the University of Massachusetts. I'd say he's safe for Aunt Grace to have as a friend."

"Well, that's good because I think Aunt Grace is interested in him as a friend."

We drove along for a few more miles. Then I said, "It's interesting that this new friend of Aunt Grace comes from Massachusetts. That's where Matt's daughter has been in school the past three years. At Amherst."

Jake said, "I didn't know your friend Matt had a daughter."

"Yes. Annette is her name. She took her first year here at Harding and then went east. Matt adores her."

"Does she come to visit him?"

"Sometimes. She hasn't been here for several months. It's easier for him to fly up there and see her. And he does. They are very close."

I smiled, thinking of her, and added, "She is a very bright girl, articulate, like her Dad. We're good friends. I tried to call her this week, but didn't get her."

He said, "That worry you?"

"Not really. She is like all college students who are busy with their own schedules. She will return my call one of these days."

The sun had gone down, and the tranquil early darkness of the Oklahoma night enveloped us. We were about halfway to Tulsa, and I saw the magic golden arches of MacDonald's, the half-way rest stop, in the distance.

He asked, "Want to stop for coffee? A coke?"

"I'll wait. A glass of wine sounds much better."

We whirled past the neon-bright oasis of MacDonald's. The light was fading rapidly, but I could still see the gaunt twisted limbs of sycamore and black jack trees outlined against the sky. I felt calmer than I had in a long time.

We rode along in a comfortable silence for a time then Jake said, "Does your friend Matt often come to Tulsa to write papers with another professor? As he was doing the night Stafford was killed?"

I said, "He was co-authoring a paper with a friend who teaches philosophy at Tulsa University. I think it was probably the first time he'd worked with someone else."

"That's interesting."

His tone nettled me. "It's not unusual. Professors collaborate all the time; that's how a lot of knowledge gets shared, you know."

He caught the annoyance in my voice, and glanced at me. "But you have to admit that it was convenient that he had such a good alibi for where he was that night. Right?"

The comfortable feeling was slipping away. I straightened up in the seat and said, with a touch of sarcasm, "Detective Fleshman, you are a *very* suspicious person. But I'm sure you checked Matt as carefully as everyone else on your list."

"Yes. And I plan to do a re-check."

"But why? Matt said he didn't leave Tulsa until after eight-thirty that evening. His friend confirmed that, and there's no way he could have driven to OK City in thirty minutes. Even in his Jag he couldn't have done that."

"No, you're right, he couldn't."

I said impatiently, "Then why bother to check him again?"

"Routine stuff, Connie."

"Routine or not, I can't imagine what motive you think Matt Duncan might have had for killing Dean Stafford."

"I don't worry too much about motive. There are all kinds of motives that cause someone to kill. What I look for is opportunity and means. That's why I'm checking Duncan's time schedule. Did he have the opportunity?"

I said, my voice showing my annoyance, "That seems irrational to me. I would be looking for someone who had the best motive. Someone more volatile and crazy -- like Boyd Finnell."

He replied, "Well, from all outward appearances, it looks like everyone who knew the Dean had a reason to want him dead, or a motive as you mention. But motive is an inward thing, and unfortunately I don't have the ability to discern the passions of people." He smiled. "Wish I did, might make my job easier."

I gazed out the window. The darkness was complete, broken only by the lights of the oncoming cars.

I said, "So it's just a matter of keeping on and sifting through alibis and any other evidence you can find."

"That's about it. Not very glamorous, and not as easy as the movies make it." He paused, then said, "But the slogging along pays off. You remember what I said about following the money trail of Munsell?"

I nodded, remembering that both he and Aunt Grace had said that money might be the reason for the death of Stafford.

"Well, I got a break. I made a couple of discreet calls to two banker friends. One of them called me back with some interesting news. Vice President Munsell has been making deposits to his bank for over three years. In addition to his regular deposits, I mean. Right now he has a tidy $300,000 in his savings account."

I said, "My God, Jake, where could Munsell have got that kind of money?"

"That's exactly what I asked. His salary wouldn't do it, but I found out that he has access to large amounts of money at the University."

"What are you talking about?"

"He is in charge of the Foundation Fund which receives millions of dollars from ex-students and benevolent corporations each year."

I said, "I know that, but he has a board he is accountable to."

"A board that meets only twice a year. Easy enough to fix a report for those two meetings."

"You think he's been stealing money from the University?"

"You tell me. The money had to come from somewhere. I'm getting a subpoena to examine the Foundation Fund records. Should have it soon. Then we will see."

I was dumbfounded. I hadn't liked Munsell, but I had never thought of him as a thief.

Jake added, "And guess who was the faculty member who helped him administer the Foundation Fund money? The late Dean Stafford. Who, by the way, was appointed about a year ago to serve in that capacity by Munsell."

I had recovered enough to stammer, "Are you saying that Munsell and Stafford were partners? In embezzling funds?"

"It's a possibility."

"That's pretty wild."

"Okay, maybe it is. But suppose that they *were* in it together and that somewhere along the line they had a falling out."

"Are suggesting that Munsell might have killed Stafford?"

He waited a minute before he answered. "Munsell admitted that he was working at the university that evening, and he was alone and no one can verify that he stayed in his office all evening. His secretary said he was there at six o'clock when she left, but that's it."

"Remember what I said about *opportunity* and *means?* He had both. He could have walked to the L.A. building, killed Stafford and been back in his office without anyone seeing him.

Except Clarence, who wouldn't have been surprised to have seen him in the building."

"But why? What was his motive?"

"If there was embezzling, how about greed? Maybe Stafford was demanding a larger cut, and Munsell didn't want to share. Maybe he could see the whole thing getting out of hand, and in a fit of anger killed him?"

A cold chill shot up my spine. What Jake said made sense. Munsell might be the killer, and if he were, he could be dangerous. And I had put pressure on him, had told him that I had a file that had something to do with Stafford.

"Jake, I . . . I began, about to tell him how I had made a deal with Munsell to get a promotion. But I stopped.

My pride kicked in. I didn't want Jake to know what I had done. I had used blackmail, plain and simple, and I was beginning to have second thoughts about the rightness of it.

In a way, I had become like Munsell and Stafford and all the rest of their kind who cheated and schemed to get what they wanted. I felt dirty, as if I had betrayed myself, and it was not a good feeling.

Jake asked, "What are you trying to say?"

"Oh, it's just that I hate thinking that someone connected with Harding is guilty of murder. It's depressing and it's frightening."

Jake's voice was contrite. "Bear with me a little longer. We'll swing by and check up on Matt's friend, and then I'll forget that I'm a cop and we'll enjoy the opera."

He added, "It's a great love story. And a tragedy."

I replied, "Most love stories are."

Chapter 29

It was Wednesday morning and I was on my way to my ten-thirty class, my mind on the examination I had scheduled. I saw Matt's broad back ahead of me and I called out, "Hey, Matt, wait up."

I wanted to ask him about Annette .He stopped and waited for me. He looked tired. "How's it going, Matt?

"All right., he said. His voice was brusque, and he seemed preoccupied, as if I'd caught him at a bad time.

"Are you okay?"

"Yes," he said, glancing away. He seemed anxious to be on his way. I didn't think he was okay. His body language was all wrong.

I tried to lighten the conversation. "Some cute co-ed giving you trouble?"

I saw immediately that I'd made a silly remark. "I'm sorry." I felt my face flushing, and I said, "What I really wanted to ask is how is Annett?'

His face changed. "She's doing good. Heard from her a couple of days ago. She had aced her final philosophy exam, the course she had to take outside her discipline.

I said. "I tried to call her, but I could not get her. Tell her hello for me."

He said, "Sure' and turned to go.

I reached out and touched his arm. "How about our trip to San Diego? I need a break, and you look like you could stand some sunshine."

His smiled, but his eyes were weary. "We'll go. Soon. I'll let you know."

Late that afternoon Jake called. "Two things to tell you," he said. "First, we got the subpoena today to check on the Foundation Fund records."

I asked, "What are you looking for?

"Anything that connects Munsell and Stafford with stealing funds."

"It's the money trail, isn't it?"

"Yes."

"I hope you and Aunt Grace are right. About finding the murderer at the end of the trail."

"I hope so too." He paused. "The second thing is that something's come up and I won't be able to take you to dinner tonight. I got a call from the sheriff in Enid. He's an old friend and he's in trouble about a prisoner who got hurt in his jail. I promised I'd come over. It will be late when I get back. Can I give you a rain check?"

"Of course," I said. I hung up the phone and sat staring into space. I hadn't realized how much I had been looking forward to having dinner with him. Was I letting my friendship with him slip over into something more personal?

I thought about the times we had been together, the trip to the lake, the visit to the Blue Boar, the opera. I reminded myself that those were friendly gestures on his part. He was just being kind, and letting me learn how a murder case works. I didn't need to flatter myself its was anything more than that.

I thought about Munsell. Was he embezzling money from the Foundation? Had Stafford been in on it with him? Was the file Munsell was so anxious to get from me part of the paper trail that would trip him up?

I picked up the papers from my last class. Since the dinner was canceled, I would stay and grade them rather than go home. That would help me get my mind off what Jake might find out about Munsell.

I picked up the first one on the stack. I sighed when I saw *it's* used as a possessive. Even advanced students had a problem with that one. The papers didn't get much better. *Would they ever stop using there for their?* Or the ambiguous *a lot* when they meant *many?*

Then, to make things worse, I found one paper written by a C student whose whole essay was compelling and flawlessly written. I groaned.

That meant only one thing. Somehow the student, an older woman, had managed to cheat, and I would have to challenge her. *Damn, damn. How could she be so stupid? Why didn't she at least change the sentences and put them into her own words?*

I took a ten minute break, propping my feet on my desk and wondering for the millionth time why someone would work so hard and spend so much time preparing to cheat on a paper. I had never been able to figure that out.

I sighed and dug back into the remaining papers. When I looked up some time later I saw that I had only thirty minutes until my late afternoon class.

Rosa was gone, but she had left the coffee pot on, and I poured a cup of the black liquid, hoping it would give me a jolt.

It did. It was bitter and strong, and I sipped it slowly, letting its warmth spread through my tired body. I was ten minutes late for the class, having had trouble finding a book of criticism I needed, but the students were patiently waiting.

I launched into our study of Robert Browning's dramatic monologues. By the time we had finished our discussion of "Porphyria's Lover" and read the weird dialog of the demented lover for the girl he had just murdered, they were hooked.

I gave them the scheduled test at the second hour. This time I kept a careful eye on them, determined I wouldn't let anyone slip in cheated answers.

Most of the students were finished by seven-thirty, but two of the older women labored over their answers until I finally told them they had ten minutes to finish.

I liked the older students, but they worried so about grades, I guess, to compensate for being older. I waited patiently.

It was five minutes of eight when the last one handed me her paper. I hurried down the hall, anxious to get away. I was tired but exhilarated as I always am after a lively class. I was also starved.

I was gathering papers and books and planning where I would stop for something to eat when someone knocked at the door. "Damn," I said, as I tossed my brief case on the desk.

I thought it was one of the nervous older women who wanted to ask a final question. I opened the door, determined to stand in the doorway and keep her out of my office.

It was Vice President Munsell. I was surprised to see him.

"Dr. Munsell," I said, stammering a bit. I wasn't expecting *you*."

"No, I'm sure you weren't, Dr. Crashaw." His eyes flitted around the room, and he nervously ran one hand over his mouth while the other hand remained in his coat pocket. He looked like a second story man caught red-handed in a robbery.

The idea was so ridiculous that in spite of myself I smiled and sat down in my chair. The smile seemed to relax him a bit, and I gestured to a chair and said, "Won't you sit down?"

He stiffened and said, "No. This won't take long. I want to let you know that I signed your promotion to full professor today and I have sent it to the President's office.

You will receive the official notice tomorrow. I've kept my part of the bargain. Now I want that file."

My heart lurched into my throat. His eyes were steely and his voice was curt. Too late I realized that I should have had something clearly in mind to tell him when he found out that I really *didn't* have a file.

I moved uncomfortably in my chair and rubbed my hands together, stalling for a moment. Then I decided that the only choice I had was to tell the truth.

I cleared my throat. "I'm sorry, Dr. Munsell, but there isn't any file. I didn't tell the truth. I wanted the promotion badly enough to deceive you . . . ."

His face darkened, and I could see the muscles in his jaw twitching. Suddenly he reached into his jacket and jerked out a small black pistol. He pointed it at me, and said, "I'm tired of dancing around with you, and I'm particularly tired of your continual lies."

He reached in his coat pocket, pulled out a folded piece of paper, and threw it on my desk. "Read it," he snapped.

The sight of a gun in his hand frightened me and I had trouble unfolding the note. When I managed to get it open, I recognized the handwriting. It was from Dean Stafford, and it was dated September 15, almost four months before he was killed.

I began to read, and I felt the muscles in my stomach knotting up. It said: "Wesley, in case you try either to cut me out of the money, or set me up as a patsy, I'm giving Connie Crashaw a detailed account of our little financial enterprise with enough documentation to keep you in prison for a very long time. It's sealed, and the good Dr. Crashaw won't open it -- unless something happens to me. Call it my fail safe plan. You needn't worry about it unless you do something stupid."

I stared at the note. This was crazy. Why would Stafford tell such a lie? Why incriminate me by suggesting I was his friend, someone he could trust?

I had no answer to those questions, but I knew one thing for sure. His note made it impossible for me to convince Munsell that I did *not* have a file.

My mind whirled, trying to get a handle on what I could do. The only thing I could think of was to stall and hope that somehow I could get away from him. .I looked up, and Munsell said, "Now don't tell me you don't have the file."

I kept my voice as calm as I could with a gun pointed at my stomach. I didn't want him to get off a nervous shot. I said, "All right. I promised the Dean to keep it secure. It's at my home."

His face turned livid. He said, "If you don't stop lying!" His finger tightened on the trigger. "I've checked out your house."

Oh my God. He was the one who had rummaged through my office -- and searched my house? He was probably the one who tried to run me into the ditch.

My heart was racing. I said, "You didn't know where to look. I have it in a wall safe in my bedroom."

He stared at me. I kept my eyes fixed on his and prayed.

Suddenly he motioned with the gun, "Then let's go."

I let out my breath, and slipped the note into my pocket. I said, "The key to unlock the safe security box is filed here. I'll need to get it."

I was hoping that someone might still be in the building, that I might be able to get away from him. I didn't want to think about what he would do when he found out I didn't have the file at home.

His voice was sharp, impatient. "Then get it now!"

I went to my personal file cabinet, and rummaged around, looking for any kind of key that I could use to show him. I finally found the file cabinet key. I held it up and said, "Here it is." I don't think I had ever been as frightened as I was at that moment. I was convinced that if I had any chance at all, I had to get away from him before we got to my house.

He said, "Let's go. You'll walk right beside me. If you see anyone, don't do anything foolish."

"There's no one here, my students are gone."

He said, "We will go to your house, I'll get the file, and we will forget this meeting ever happened."

You are lying. You will kill me just like you did Stafford and Clarence.

In the hallway he kept me slightly ahead of him, holding my arm firmly. When we got outside, I glanced around, praying that a late departing student might see us. But no one was in sight. The parking lot was practically deserted, only three or four cars were in sight. I was shivering, more from the tension than the cold. A mist was falling and the temperature had dropped. I almost stumbled as we walked down the sidewalk which was icing over.

We approached my car and Munsell said, "You'll drive." But before he could shove me inside, a man got out of one of the cars and started toward us.

He said, "Keep quiet, ignore him and get in the car." He thrust me out a little ahead of him, but his hand was tight on my arm. The gun was pressing against my back. I stumbled, and he had to catch me, giving the man time to get closer.

It was Jake.

My heart began to pound. Something had brought him back from Enid. Would he realize that something was wrong?

He was almost upon us when Munsell hissed in my ear, "Get rid of him."

Fleshman stopped and said, "Glad I caught you, Dr. Crashaw. Looks like we can have dinner after all." He was looking at me, but I couldn't be sure that he would see the fear in my face.

I had only a split second to make a decision. I said, "Sorry, I can't. We're going to get the Stafford file that Dr. Munsell has been asking about." Then I jerked my arm and spun away from Munsell. My foot hit the ice, and my feet flew out from under me. In the second before I hit the ground, I saw Jake crouching, a gun in his hand, and I heard shots.

I hit the ground hard. I bounced on my shoulder and sprawled awkwardly with my hands out in front of me. Instinctively I rolled, scrabbling on my knees to get as far away from the gunshots as I could.

Then I saw someone looming over me, and for a split second I thought it was Munsell. I screamed. Then the person was holding me tightly and saying, "It's okay, it's okay. You're all right now."

It was Jake.

Chapter **30**

Only gradually did I become calm enough for Jake to pull me to my feet. Even then I was shaking so that I wasn't sure I could walk. He helped me into his car, and turned on the motor. "I've got to call in. Will you be all right?"

I nodded, unable to do any better than that. I felt frozen to the core, and I pulled my coat closer around me. The car heater was going full blast, but it didn't seem to help. I didn't think I would ever be warm again.

I heard Jake calling for police backup and an ambulance. Minutes later I saw the red and white lights of incoming police cars and heard the wail of an ambulance in the distance.

I said, "Where's Munsell? What happened?"

Jake opened the car door. "It's okay. Just stay here."

He slammed the door and walked toward the two police cars that had pulled up. The policemen, guns drawn, jumped out.

"Over here," Jake said, motioning. "We've got one down over here."

The ambulance, lights flashing, maneuvered into place alongside the police cars. I watched as they took a stretcher and hurried to where Jake and the policemen stood. They picked Munsell up and placed him on the stretcher.

I needed to find out how badly Munsell had been hurt. I had heard shots and he had fallen shortly after I had fallen. My hands were trembling so badly I had difficulty opening the car door, but I finally managed to get one foot outside.

Jake saw me and motioned me back.

He said something to one of the officers and hurried over.

"Stay inside the car, Connie. Everything's under control." His body was blocking my view of what was happening.

"What about Munsell?"

"He's dead."

"Oh my God."

Jake leaned over and looked directly at me. "I had no choice. He shot first."

"Oh God, Jake."

I felt sick. *Munsell dead? Was it my fault?* I had let him believe I had a file because I had been determined to get a promotion. I had deliberately lied to him about the whole thing. And now he was dead.

Jake was asking me something about Munsell. "What happened here? "Why was Munsell holding a gun on you?"

I was finding it difficult to breathe. What could I say?

"Connie?"

I can't tell him that I lied to Munsell. I fumbled in my pocket. "Here," I said, thrusting the Stafford note at him.

He looked at me briefly, then he began to read.

"I'll be damned," he said. "So this is why he was so sure you had a file." He paused. "He had come to get it?"

I didn't answer.

"And you were taking him to your house? Did you tell him it was there?"

My heart was pounding. I stuttered, "I was stalling him. I was trying to think of how I could get away from him."

"He might have killed you."

I took a deep breath. "Is it over?"

"This is over."

"No, I mean, did Munsell kill Stafford?"

He looked puzzled, as if I had asked a stupid question. "It looks like it. If we find hard evidence of Munsell embezzling and Stafford involved, and I think we will, I would say yes.

Then you and Aunt Grace were right -- it was the money. Suddenly I was exhausted, and I wanted to get away from everything. From Jake. From his questioning.

I needed time to get my mind around all that had happened. But I didn't think I could drive my car so I said, "Can you drive me home?"

"Of course, just wait a minute." He called to one of the uniformed officers, told him to secure the scene. He said to him, "I'll be back in thirty minutes" and slid in beside me.

He backed the car out cautiously. A sheet of ice had crystallized on the parking lot, turning it into a treacherous slippery surface.

We eased carefully out of the parking lot and I glanced at him. The bright moonlight filled the car with a soft white light that etched the lines in his face and haloed his hair, chiseling him into a dark statue.

My head was throbbing and my stomach was queasy, and I didn't think I could utter a coherent sentence, but my mind wouldn't shut down.

From somewhere out of my subconscious, one of Aunt Grace's warnings floated into my mind. I could hear her saying "Be sure your sins will find you out, Constance. Whatever you sow, that is what you will reap." It had been a part of her never-ending counsel during my rebellious teenage years.

She had been right. My lie to Munsell was going to bear bitter fruit. I would forever wonder if I had been partly responsible for his death. What would Jake think when he found out that I had been blackmailing Munsell?

"Jake," I began . . . and stopped. I did not have the courage to continue. My need to protect myself, to rationalize my actions took charge.

I looked away. I don't have to tell him. What good would it do? Nothing I can say will change what has happened in the last two hours.

"What?" he said.

I looked at him and asked, "Are you all right?"

"Yes," he said. "What I had to do . . . it's part of my job. I'm a cop."

I sank deeper into the car seat, wanting to disappear completely.

A few minutes later we pulled up into my driveway. He cut the ignition and said, "Look. He had a gun, he shot at me. I had no choice but to shoot back. He's responsible for his death." He looked tired. This whole thing had been a nightmare for him as well as for me.

I slid toward the door, opened it and got out. I stood beside the car for a moment. Then I said, "It's a terrible world we live in." The words sounded hollow and trivial even as I said them.

His response was simple. "You're right." He waited until I walked to the house and went inside. Then I heard the sound of his car leaving.

Wearily I locked the door behind me and walked slowly down the hallway. Tess appeared out of my bedroom, her eyes wide and questioning -- and reproachful.

Knowing she was hungry, I walked to the kitchen, opened a can and put the food in her bowl. She gave me a grateful look before she began to eat.

I sat at the kitchen table watching her for a minute. Then I microwaved a cup of morning coffee and sat back down. I reached over and rubbed her. She arched her back against my hand but kept on eating.

I said, "Am I a monster, Tess? I did what everybody else on the frigging faculty does. I turned an opportunity to my advantage; I manipulated someone into giving me a promotion."

I took a sip of coffee; it was bitter.

I continued talking. "For eight long years, I did all the right things, and I never got a raise or a promotion. I saw young men get the promotions -- for no good reason -- except for the good ole boy system at work. So when I had a chance to beat it, I took it."

Tess looked up from eating. Her glance seemed accusing.

"I. . . I. . ."The tears began slowly, silently. I wiped them away, but they didn't stop. My throat hurt.

I clung to the edge of the table. The reality of all that happened seemed to be weighting down on my shoulders, and my mind was in chaos.

I heard myself saying, " *God. Oh God,*" which was a kind of desperate prayer.

I had finally stepped over the edge. I had become as deceitful and selfishly manipulative as the college administrators I despised. But I was worse than any of them. Their lies only made people miserable; my lies had killed a man.

When I was finally able to stop the tears, Tess was rubbing up against my legs and meowing plaintively. I picked her up and walked into the bedroom. I sat on the bed, and Tess flattened out beside me.

I was desperately tired, and my emotions were raw.

I thought *"I can resign, move away. Get out of the teaching profession altogether. But if I tell Jake. . . .*

"No matter,"I said.

"I've got to tell him."

Chapter **31**

The next morning my body felt like I had been pummeled by some malevolent monster out of one of Grimm's fairy tales. My head throbbed.

I raised my body up slowly, and carefully pivoted my head from right to left to see if my neck muscles were working. They were, though painfully, and I eased out of bed and headed for the bathroom to get something for the aching.

I swallowed two Tylenol, splashed water on my face, and glanced at myself in the mirror. Not a pretty sight. My left cheek was turning purple where I had landed on it, and I had a considerable knot on my forehead. I looked quickly away.

I wobbled my way down the hallway to the kitchen. I couldn't separate the pounding headache from the noise of the gunshots still echoing in my head.

How many shots had I heard? I couldn't remember. The panic and fear of that split second of jerking away from Munsell swept over me again. I remembered hitting the icy pavement, completely out of control, and skidding and rolling before I stopped. Out of the corner of my eye, I had seen Munsell fall.

He's dead.

Trembling, I sat down at the kitchen table, willing my heart to slow down. I wanted coffee desperately, but I was not sure I could handle the coffee maker.

I managed to open the instant coffee, and poured hot water from the tap over it and stirred it up. But the taste was terrible. It was not only weak, but also tepid,

I popped the cup into the microwave oven, but left it too long, and it boiled over. I didn't have the energy or inclination to start over, so I swilled down the half cup that was left.

I thought about the decision I had made last night. I had to tell Jake the reason Munsell had been holding a gun on me.

In the bleak morning light, my doubts and fears resurfaced, and to tell Jake it didn't seem such a good idea this morning. But I still felt uncomfortable -- and guilty about the whole thing.

The phone jangled and I jumped, knocking over the dregs of my coffee. I grabbed the phone. "Hello,"

Jake said, "How're you doing?"

"Okay," I stammered. It was unnerving to have him call just as I was thinking of whether I would tell him about my lie to Munsell.

His voice was sympathetic. "You don't sound too good."

"I'm not going to work today."

"A good idea. I'm not either."

"What's happening with you?"

"You mean about the shooting?"

I hadn't meant that, but I said, "Yes."

"Routine procedure. I'm suspended until I get an all clear. That it was a good shoot."

"Oh." *What the hell is a good shoot? How could killing a man ever be called a good shoot?*

A long, uncomfortable silence followed.

Then I said, "Would you stop by for coffee?" I might as well face him and decide, once and for all, if I wanted to tell him about the lie.

"I can be there in thirty minutes."

I had to get dressed, but the palms of my hands were bruised from my skid on the hard surface of the parking lot, making it difficult to handle anything.

It took me the full thirty minutes to get into jeans and a T shirt, wash my face and brush my hair. I was awkward and stiff, and everything I did required a great deal of energy.

Tess had ambled into the bedroom, and I was heading toward the kitchen to feed her when the doorbell rang.

Jake was brushing snow off when I opened the door. Taking his heavy woolen jacket, I pointed him toward the kitchen. "I finally got the coffee pot to working. It should be ready by now."

I paused before the open door. I hadn't known that new snow was falling, but it had already powdered the yard and driveway with a clean sheet of white. The air was metallic sharp and the sky a heavy gray.

The snow would probably fall all day, covering the dirty landscape with a coat of pure white. The ice would encapsulate the trees and bushes with a glittering sheath. The cold, icy wind would cleanse the air. It was Nature's way of hiding the unsightly and marred landscape.

Another troubling thought entered my mind. *If only it could purify the human heart.*

Jake had gone into the kitchen.

I followed him shortly, poured coffee, and sat down.

He said, "I got some interesting information this morning from the auditors checking the Foundation fund."

I took a sip of coffee. Waited.

Jake said, "They found that ten automobiles belonging to the Foundation had been sold, but there was no record of what happened to the money."

He paused, waiting for my response.

I managed to say, "Interesting."

"More than that. A dozen cash scholarships never got to students, and a $50,000 Mobil Oil gift to be used for handicapped students was cashed by Munsell."

"So Munsell *was* embezzling funds." My voice sounded hollow and flat.

"Yes. And Stafford was in on it.. Munsell allotted the scholarships to Liberal Arts, and Stafford awarded them to non-existent students, which meant he put the money in his pocket.

The fifty thousand Mobil oil gift was apparently split between them."

"I never pictured the Dean as a thief."

"Apparently he had expensive tastes."

I knew that was true.

I remembered all the times he had bragged to me about attending the premier of a New York play and staying at the Waldorf. And how he had often wined and dined at Ciro's.

I thought of the countless the parties he had attended in the City, squiring rich socialites around. He had to have been spending chunks of money to keep up his lifestyle.

I said, 'But if they had a good thing going, why would Munsell kill the Dean?"

"Who knows? Greed? Maybe he wanted all the money for himself. Or maybe he was afraid that Stafford would turn on him. Or maybe they just got into an argument that accelerated and erupted into a fatal fight."

"But why kill Clarence?"

"Because he happened to see Munsell that night."

"Do you think that Clarence must have said something to Munsell about seeing him leave the building."

Jake shrugged. "Something like that, I suppose."

I didn't say anything for several seconds. The whole depressing scenario had simply overwhelmed me. Then I thought about the condoms and asked, "But why the condoms? That doesn't make any sense."

"Ever hear of a red herring? I think Munsell put them there to make it look like a sexually motivated murder. From what you have said, apparently the dean had enough affairs to make him a likely victim. What better way to divert suspicion than to make it look like it was the result of an affair gone wrong?"

"Then the case is closed?"

"I think so."

A picture of Wilma Munsell, small and drab in a dark gray suit, flashed into my mind. I had seen her only occasionally at faculty gatherings and she seemed always to be wearing something gray.

I said, "I'm sorry for his wife. What will happen to her?"

"There's no evidence she had any knowledge of the embezzling. There will be some kind of accounting of what money is legitimately hers, and then my guess is that she will take it and leave."

"The whole thing is like something out of a Hawthorne novel."

"This is the real world," he said, his voice subdued.

"Then I think I'm ready to stop the world and get off."

"No place to go."

"You're right. And that's the hell of it."

We sat silent for a long time. He took a long drink of coffee. "You were gutsy last night, taking the chance you did when you jerked away from Munsell."

"I was scared out of my wits."

"Stafford set you up when he sent Munsell that note. You could have been killed."

I thought about Munsell's fury, the gun, the narrow margin of sanity that kept him from shooting me in my office.

"Yes," I said, "I guess so."

"Strange that Stafford would set you up like that."

I shrugged. "If you're asking me *why*, I can't tell you. . ." My voice trailed off.

"Munsell was certainly convinced that Dean Stafford had sent you a file that would destroy him."

"Yes," I said. "But there is something that I must tell you." I paused. "Something else you need to know, Jake."

He was looking intently at me.

I dropped my eyes and gazed at my hands, trying to stop their trembling. I said, "I told Munsell a week ago that I had the file he was looking for. I lied to him. And I used the lie to force Munsell to promote me to full professor." He had come to my office to tell me the promotion had gone through. He had kept his part of the bargain, and he wanted the file."

The silence was loud, the atmosphere heavy.

Jake was staring at me. He said, "Blackmail is always dangerous, Connie. You back someone into a corner and that makes for a desperate person."

"I know. And it was wrong as well."

A slight smile edged his lips. "You're right, and now you're feeling guilty. About Munsell's death?"

I nodded.

"You got caught in a trap. Dean Stafford set you up. Remember?"

"Yes, but I. . . ."

"Look, Connie, deal with your guilt however you can. I'm not a priest, and I can't help you there.

"But don't beat yourself to death about Munsell. He was on a collision course and he was responsible for putting himself there."

For a minute, I wanted to agree with Jake's evaluation of the situation. I wanted to find some way of making my actions seem not so bad and what he was saying made some kind of bizarre sense.

But I had been too thoroughly and religiously trained by Aunt Grace in what was right and wrong to be able to let myself off the hook so easily.

I said, "You are right about Munsell, but what I did in trying to get myself promoted was not right." I wanted to ease both the tension and the seriousness of the discussion, and put the whole thing behind me if I could.

I managed a slight smile and said, "But I am a product of Aunt Grace's moral and religious training, and she has said to me a thousand times at least that I'm responsible for whatever I do. Rationalizing doesn't play well with her either."

"She is a wise lady," he said, his face serious and intent. Then he added, "Let it go, Connie, you did what you had to do."

I didn't know anything else to say but "Thanks for listening to me ,Jake."

"No problem." He glanced at his watch. "Got to go. Will I see you later?"

"Yes," I said.

After Jake left, I felt better, but I was still restless. I decided a walk might help clear my thoughts, and erase the uneasiness that still hung heavily on.me.

I went out outside through the back door, and headed toward the creek bed. The snow fell gently and cooled my face. I trudged along, cocooned in the quiet whiteness, trying to come to terms with myself.

The thought of resigning from the University and striking out on my own suddenly became very appealing. I *could* leave. I was responsible for no one but myself.

But where would I go? What could I do? I didn't have any skills other than teaching. I was confused and felt particularly helpless.

Finally, I turned around and headed back toward the house, facing the wind which had become stronger. I walked as fast as I could against its strength, trying to move faster toward the warmth and comfort of my kitchen again.

When I finally got to the back door and opened it, I heard my answering machine beeping. I hurried to pick up the phone.

It was Matt, wanting me to call. Chilled from the cold, I went into the den and sat before the fireplace for about ten minutes. Then I picked up the phone and dialed his number.

He answered on the second ring. "I heard about what happened. Are you all right?"

Not really. Not worth a damn. "I'm okay."

"What did happen? Why were you with Munsell anyhow?"

"It's a long story, Matt. Bottom line is he thought I had something, a file, that would prove he was embezzling money from the University."

"Did you? Have a file?"

"No."

"Sorry. Didn't mean to pry."

"Didn't mean to snap at you. It's just that I'm weary and half-way crazy about all that happened."

"Good reason to be." His voice was warm and comforting.

I said, "Things worked out. Jake thinks the murders are solved."

"Glad to hear that. Now maybe he'll get off my case."

"What do you mean?"

"He's been questioning Tony again. About the exact time I left Tulsa that Sunday."

He paused, and then added. "And get this: the Headmistress at Holyoke called me a couple of days ago. Fleshman was asking questions about Annette."

His voice roughened. "Which is none of his damn business."

"I know," I said. I understood Matt's anger.

"And we both need a change. So we're leaving tomorrow morning."

"Tomorrow's Friday, Matt. What about classes?"

"Screw 'em. I've got clearance at the airport for seven a.m."

I liked the idea. It was time to do something different. "You're right. I'll go. Screw the whole damn University."

"That's my girl. I'll pick you up at six-thirty."

Chapter 32

Matt's Learjet sat on the tarmac at Wiley Post airport, sleek and silver, glistening in the early morning sun. He pulled up alongside it and we got out.

I was thankful that Matt was rich, that he was my dear friend, and that he was getting me away from all that had happened.

"It's a great day for flying," Matt said as he opened the door to the plane.

"Couldn't be better." I replied.

He loaded our luggage, and I slid into the seat next to him in the cockpit. The soft leather seat was warm from the sun and I relaxed while he did his pre-flight check.

We lifted off shortly after seven. There seemed to be no wind blowing which is rare in Oklahoma.

Behind a few puffy clouds in the east, the sun pinked the sky, the harbinger of a clear, beautiful day. I was both exhilarated and peaceful.

I looked up into the blue sky where only a few white clouds drifted along, and sighed. There is something ethereal and otherworldly about lifting off from the earth and heading into the sunlight. I am always amazed at the limitless blue space and the sense of wonder I feel.

I've never been able to be blasé about flying. I said, "If we keep flying west, we can always keep the darkness behind us, can't we?"

Matt smiled. "I don't know if we can fly that fast, or even if we want to. The darkness is sometimes comfortable, maybe even necessary." He understood what I was talking about. He always did.

"Maybe so," I said. "I expect you're right." It was good to get away, both from the ice and snow and the disturbing events of the past weeks.

I placed my hand on his shoulder, and briefly rubbed his neck. I said, "I called Aunt Grace late last evening and told her that we were going to San Diego for two days."

"And she said. . .?"

"She didn't say anything, but she wasn't too pleased." I glanced at Matt. "It goes against all her religious principles for two unmarried people to be spending a weekend together."

He laughed.

"I told her we were staying at the Del Coronado and that we would have separate rooms.

"What was her response to that?"

"Something like 'harrumph,' which translated means 'I don't want to talk about it.'

I also tried to call Detective Fleshman, but got his answering machine."

Matt frowned. "Why did you call him?"

"I don't know, I guess I thought he might need me as a witness. About Munsell's death, I mean."

"I imagine he can take care of that situation."

"Probably. He's very good at what he does."

I leaned back against the leather seat and glanced at Matt again. His face, outlined against the window, was intent. He was concentrating on getting the plane to its proper cruising altitude.

He was a competent flyer and a cautious one, and I always felt safe with him. He focused on his flying until he leveled the plane off to its cruising altitude. Then he winked at me and said, "We're okay. Relax and enjoy the scenery."

The squared fields over which we were flying looked like a huge green-and-brown pieced quilt. The sun bronzed the small ponds, making them look like golden doubloons scattered by a careless pirate.

"It's beautiful," I said.

"And peaceful. Up here everything is clean and clear and right."

"Makes you want to take off and never come back, doesn't it?"

He smiled. "We could do that. Just refuel at San Diego and fly south or west until we found a Shangri-La that suited us. Leave academia forever. Loll on a beach and read pop novels and sage philosophers."

I stretched my arms above my head and said, "Sounds heavenly."

"Marry me, Con."

His voice was serious, but at first I thought he was teasing me. I glanced at him again. His face was as serious as his voice.

I decided to be casual about the whole thing. I said, "Okay, Dr. Duncan. You've got a deal. We can detour to Las Vegas, get a quickie marriage at one of the 'marrying Sam' chapels. It would be fun."

"I'm serious."

I laughed. "Oh, <u>sure</u> you are. But one thing before we go any further. I insist on a pre-nuptial agreement, I'd say . . . about a million dollars would do nicely. Just in case, you know."

"Look at me, Connie."

I was smiling, but there was no laughter in his face. "We could be happy. You'd have anything you want."

I had never seen such intensity in his eyes, and it surprised me. I said, "You're kidding, of course."

"No. I mean it. Will you marry me?"

I had to take a minute. He *was* serious.

I had always loved Matt for all the things he had done for me, the support he had given, his unselfish friendship, but I had never thought of marrying him. And it had never occurred to me that he would want me to marry him.

I said, very carefully, "But, Matt, I don't love you, you don't love me . . . I mean, we love each other, but not like that."

"Not like what?" He paused. "We lived together for months, we made love, we shared with each other. What else is there?"

I was rattled. I tried to think of how to explain what he surely already knew. But we're not *in love,* Matt; you know that."

"Then maybe I don't know what being *in love* means. I know I love being with you, I trust you, I respect you. "

I interrupted, trying to lessen the fervor of what he was saying. "And the sex was great, don't forget that."

He smiled. That too. So why not marry me?"

"Because. Because it wouldn't work. We're friends, Matt, good friends, the best of friends, but after a time we wouldn't be."

"I'm not going back, Con."

There was such bleak despair in his voice that I was frightened. *What did he mean he was not going back?*

"What are you talking about?"

"Fleshman knows about Annette, and eventually he'll put it all together."

My heart began to beat faster. "Knows what about Annette? Put what together?"

There was a long silence. My brain raced as I thought of what might be wrong. What kind of trouble was Annette in? Had Jake found out something about her? Was she into drugs? Was she pregnant?

The muscles in Matt's his jaws were rigid, and when he looked at me again, tears were gleaming in his eyes. My heart began to pound. In all the years I had known him, I had never seen him cry.

"What is it?"

"Annette is sick, Connie. About a month ago . . . she had a mental breakdown. She's in a hospital in Boston." His voice stumbled. "She's. . . she doesn't even recognize me.'

I was having trouble taking in what he was saying, and I stuttered, "What are you talking about? What happened?"

Again, a long silence. I could feel his anguish as he struggled for control. He set the plane on automatic pilot, and faced me.

His eyes were those of a man who has peered into the abyss and seen his own personal hell. His voice was low and he spoke slowly, as if each word were painful to utter. "She got pregnant - last spring - she had an abortion."

"Oh God, Matt. Not Annette!"

"She couldn't handle the trauma, the guilt after the abortion. She kept saying she had murdered her baby. In spite of all I could do, she began the slide into a psychotic break."

I didn't know what to say. I thought of the young man she had dated last spring -- Joe, Joe. . . I couldn't remember his last name.

He had probably insisted she get an abortion.

The thought made me so angry that I could barely control my voice when I said, "Who was it, Matt? That damn student Joe. . . ?"

Matt's face had become like granite, but voice was controlled. He said, "No, it wasn't a student."

"Then who?"

"Phillip Stafford."

He paused for an instant. Then he said, very deliberately, "That's why I killed him."

For a moment I felt as if I had been spun off into space, without any kind of breathing mechanism. I sat, stunned, looking at Matt. He didn't speak, and I couldn't. When I finally sucked in enough air, all I could do was repeat what he had said. "You killed Stafford?"

"I went to talk to him at the University that Sunday night. To tell him what had happened to Annette. To see if he had any remorse, felt any guilt at all." The passion in his voice was frightening.

"Do you want to know what he did?"

Matt's voice was shaking.

He said, "The fool laughed and said, 'It's too bad she didn't tell me she wasn't protecting herself,'"

Then he pulled out a handful of condoms, threw them on his desk, and said, "I'd have used these if I'd known."

"That's when I hit him. I smashed his face with my fist and when he fell, I grabbed that statue and beat his head into a pulp."

"I killed him. And I'd do it again."

The intensity of his fury filled the plane like some poisonous fog. I sat numbed, as if someone had shot my body full of a heavy narcotic.

When I could think clearly again, I began to wonder if his grief over Annette had driven him over the edge. What he was saying didn't make sense. He had been in Tulsa, writing a paper with Tony Lucas that night.

I said, "I don't believe you, Matt. You couldn't have killed Stafford. Tony swore you were with him until 8:00. You couldn't have driven to the city in thirty minutes."

"I left Tony's house at 7:00, not 8:00. Tony never looks at a clock, doesn't even own a watch. He had no idea what time it was. I left at 7:00; I told him it was 8:00."

His voice hardened. "I killed Stafford, and I'm not sorry."

I began to feel sick. If Matt had killed Stafford, he had been the "sailor" Clarence had seen, and he had killed Clarence!

Matt saw the change on my face, read my mind. "No, you've got that wrong. I didn't kill Clarence."

He reached for my hand, but I shrank away.

"Listen to me. You have got to listen to me. It was an accident. I had hired Clarence to clean out my attic, and while he was rummaging around he found the damned pea coat. I was in the attic with him, and he came to me with it in his hand and said, "It was you I seen."

I reached for the coat, and he got scared. He turned to run, slipped in those damn boots, and fell head first down the whole flight of stairs. He broke his neck. He was dead when I got to him. There was nothing I could do."

I found it hard to speak. "But why move him, Matt? How could you . . . ?"

"I panicked I guess. I didn't think; I just did it." He looked at me, misery in his face, and I knew he was telling the truth.

I said, "But you let everyone believe that Munsell killed Stafford."

"I had nothing to do with that. After Munsell was killed, everyone just *assumed* that he was the one who had killed Stafford. I just let it go. I let them believe whatever they wanted to. Munsell was dead. Nothing would bring him back. What would you have done in my place?"

There was nothing I could say. I had lied to Munsell for my own selfish reasons, and because I had lied, he had been killed, and try as hard as I could to rationalize the whole thing, I would always live with the shadow of his death over me.

Matt had turned off the automatic pilot and he was flying the plane again. I looked out the window and was shocked to see the sun shining brightly.

The whole universe should be plunged into darkness.

Finally I said, "Why are you telling me this now?"

"I don't know. Maybe because I had to tell someone about Annette. About *why* I killed Stafford. Maybe because I thought you loved me enough to marry me."

"What are you going to do?"

"I'm leaving the country."

"But what about Annette?"

His jaws tightened. "She's never going to be any better. I have made arrangements for her care. That's all I can do."

"She will need her father."

His eyes filled. "She doesn't even know me, Con. She doesn't respond to anything I say."

I saw the agony in his eyes. I had seen the devastation in his face when he had talked about losing his wife Nikki. But this pain was beyond that.

My heart sank. "What do you want from me?"

He paused and searched my face.

"It's simple, Con, we are on our way to El Paso. I will need to refuel there to be able to go on to Mexico. I will leave you in El Paso, and I will need two hours after that to sit the plane down in Mexico City. Then I'll be out of your life forever."

"Do I have a choice, Matt? I can't jump out of the plane."

"When we stop in El Paso, I'll have to trust you while we are there."

"Why didn't you just fly away by yourself?"

"Because I hoped. . . I wanted you to go with me. . . I believed that you might."

I thought about the irony of it all. I had told Jake about Annette, asked him to check on her because I was worried about her. And when he did, because he was a good detective, he had continued to check on Matt.

And Matt had panicked and fled.

Now I had to decide what I would do.

How could I possibly turn Matt in? Matt had stood by me when Eric abandoned me. His concern had kept me sane. He had supported me in every bad moment of my life. How could I refuse him now? What good would it do? The Dean was dead, and so was Munsell. Nothing could change that.

But Matt is a murderer.

"It's up to you, Con," I heard Matt saying.

I looked at him, my heart breaking.

"We'll be landing in El Paso in fifteen minutes. You'll have to decide."

El Paso, a dusty city spread out at the base of the Franklin Mountains, and nudging the border of Mexico, appeared on the horizon. Matt got clearance to land, and he guided the plane to a perfect touchdown. As he taxied up to a parking ramp, he said, "It'll take about thirty to forty-five minutes to refuel. We'll have time to get something to eat."

He parked, opened the cabin door and climbed out. As he reached up to help me, a gasoline truck pulled up alongside and two men jumped out. One of them tipped his cap and said, "We'll have you ready to roll soon."

Matt and I, silent, walked across the tarmac toward the terminal building. When we reached the building, Matt opened the door and waited for me to enter. He smiled and said, "You look like you need food and drink."

He pointed and said, "The restaurant is to our left." His voice was gentle, and his hand on my arm was light, comforting. It hardly seemed possible that minutes ago he had been telling me about Annette, about killing Stafford. The whole thing seemed unreal, like a bad dream.

The restaurant was cool and darkened against the brilliant sun. It was early for lunch, but already several tables were filled. We sat down at a table near the broad, plate glass windows.

I looked around. *All I have to do is get up and walk away. He won't stop me if I do.*

A waiter approached. Matt smiled and said, "Coffee, Con?"

I nodded, and waited until the waiter returned with the coffee and took our order before I spoke. Then I said quietly, "Why did you <u>kill</u> him, Matt? Why didn't you go through the courts, bring charges against him?"

Matt's eyes were bleak. He said, "I tried that once, remember? When the drunk teenager ran a stop light and killed Nikki? He got a fine and a suspended sentence."

"But Matt. . . ."

He reached over and placed his hand over mine. "He destroyed Annette. I couldn't let him get away with that."

"But what kind of life will you have, always on the run?"

"My life is a shambles; it's never going to be any better. The most I can hope for are a few years of solitude and peace. Is that too much to ask?"

"I don't know," I said.

The waiter brought our food, but I couldn't eat. My throat ached and my heart felt as if it were being squeezed by an iron hand. Matt was not doing any better with his food. The waiter finally came and cleared the table. We sat looking at each other over coffee, just as we had so many times. I looked into Matt's eyes, and I didn't know what to say.

He started to say something to me, but before he could, the man servicing his plane came up and said, "You're ready to go."

Matt thanked him and stood up. He said, "Two hours, Con?"

He looked at me another long moment and smiled. "I love you," he said. He turned and walked away.

Sitting very still, I watched him leave.

Dear Matt. Dear God. Why?

The waiter brought more coffee, asked if I wanted dessert. "No," I said. "I just want to sit here a while longer." I looked at the restaurant clock on the wall. It was only 12:30, only five hours since we had left Oklahoma City. It seemed eons ago that I had clambered so happily out of Matt's Jag and hurried with him to his plane.

The ground under me had shifted; my whole life had changed in that brief time. Two hours, Matt had said. He needed two hours. I sat quietly drinking coffee, barely conscious of people coming and going. At one point, the thought that I should go and arrange for a flight back to Oklahoma City flitted through my mind, but it didn't seem terribly important.

The waiter came back, asked if I would like a fresh coffee and I said yes and ordered apple pie. He brought it to me and smiled. I smiled back and thanked him.

The coffee was hot and pungent; I pushed the pie around with my fork.

A young woman with dark hair and dark eyes, probably the manager, began to raise the blinds on the windows, and I saw that the sun had disappeared behind dark thunder clouds. In a few minutes the faint patter of rain began, increasing until the windows were streaming with rivulets of water.

I looked at the clock; it was 1:30. I could feel my heart beating, and I could count the seconds ticking away with each beat. Matt needed one more hour. All I have to do is sit here one more hour, I thought. I don't have to do anything. It is not my responsibility. I don't have to make a choice.

But of course I do. If I do nothing, I am making a choice. A choice to protect Matt. If I do nothing, I am deciding to let him get away with murder.

But what happened to Annette is worse than murder. It is a living death. I don't want to decide. But I have to. And I'll have to live with the consequences.

I sat there for twenty more minutes. It was 1:50 when I stood up, paid my bill and left the restaurant. I walked out of the terminal, and stood for a moment under the portico where taxis lined the street. I looked up at the sky. The rain had stopped. The clouds were still dark and heavy. There was no wind, but the air was cold and penetrating.

Would it ever be spring again?

I turned up the collar of my coat and tightened my belt. The sidewalk stretched out before me. A few pedestrians were hurrying along, and I joined them, walking slowly. I would walk the streets of El Paso for one more hour.

Then I would phone Jake.

About the Author

Dr. Marie Saunders is a retired English teacher, living in Grapevine, Texas. She taught in the English Department of the University of Central Oklahoma, Edmond, Oklahoma for twenty-five years. After her retirement, she returned to the University and taught "Writing the Novel" in the Creative Studies Department.

Made in the USA
Charleston, SC
15 February 2013